ALOE MAN

PALMETTO
PUBLISHING
Charleston, SC
www.PalmettoPublishing.com

Copyright © 2024 by Richard Michael Barrett

All rights reserved

No portion of this book may be reproduced, stored in a retrieval system, or transmitted in any form by any means—electronic, mechanical, photocopy, recording, or other—except for brief quotations in printed reviews, without prior permission of the author.

Paperback ISBN: 979-8-8229-5005-4

ALOE MAN

A NOVEL BY

RICHARD MICHAEL BARRETT

CHAPTER ONE

Ray pulled the covers over his head and plugged his ears to muffle the annoying sound of a metal spoon banging on a cast iron skillet.

"Awwwright, guys, it's time to rise and shine!" came a screeching voice in the distance.

It belonged to an over-anxious, pimply-faced teen counselor at Camp Socketawaya, a remote summer retreat located in the backwaters of Pennsylvania's Pocono Mountains.

The high-pitched shrieking continued.

"C'mon, let's get moving, boys. We've got a big day ahead of us!!"

Those encouraging words resounded through the cabin and struck Ray's ears like fingernails on a blackboard.

"Everybody get washed up and dressed, and then meet me in the dining hall in 30 minutes. And don't be late! Now, let's move it!"

The clock on the bunk house wall read 5:30 and Ray rarely rose before 9 or 10 at home. He wasn't liking this camp thing already, and it was only the first day. He rubbed his eyes and quietly thought begging his parents to send him to summer camp may have been a mistake.

He and the other dozen kids he was bunking with had no idea what was in store but they would all find out at breakfast. Ray didn't know any of these boys since this was his first summer away. He overheard a few of them talking about their adventures last year, so he assumed they were returning campers. Ray was a tenderfoot, so he just put his head down, went about his business and didn't talk. None of them spoke to him either.

They all crowded into the wash room and carried out their respective routines as best they could, despite being away from home and not having the same familiar environment and accouterments for their morning toilette.

Ray hadn't experienced anything like this before. Multiple toilets were flushing, a cacophony of farts echoed off the tiled walls, it reeked, and a big long mirror reflected a row of guys who were elbow to elbow washing their faces, spitting out toothpaste into a sink, and combing their hair. He never had to share a bathroom with so many people before and wondered if he could ever adjust. How would he feel making his first bowel movement with a fellow camper on either side with whom he would be spending the days and weeks ahead? He told himself it would just have to wait another day to find out. He wasn't quite ready to make that leap yet and drop his first deuce.

The group trudged back to the cabin, still half-asleep, got dressed in their everyday official camp attire – gym shorts, t-shirt, sox and sneakers – and walked the short trail to the dining hall. They casually filtered in and took their places in the food line, waiting their turn to be served cafeteria-style.

Not knowing when he might eat next, Ray chose to go full-on grand slam for his first breakfast, which included scrambled eggs, a couple of strips of bacon, home fries, and a stack of buckwheat pancakes with sausage links. At the beverage station, he added an orange juice and a tall glass of chocolate milk. He noticed a few kids looking at his loaded tray, then at him, and he started to feel a little self-conscious. He didn't want to have a reputation for being a chow hound, but he was also starved.

The counselor assigned to Ray's group introduced himself as Devon and welcomed them aboard for three whole weeks of fun and games in the great outdoors. He promised there will be cool things to do, like swimming, fishing, canoeing, hiking, and archery during the day, and at night, gazing at the stars through a telescope, gathering around a campfire, singing songs and telling stories. For most young boys and teens, that sounded appealing.

Hailing from the densely populated northern New Jersey suburbs, Ray hadn't been exposed much to the outdoors. His parents, Myrna and Sol, rarely took him and his brother, Simon, and sister Bonnie Lee, anywhere for fun. He felt slightly anxious about his ability to prove that he wasn't an uncoordinated dork. He played Little League baseball and Pop Warner football and was regarded by his coaches and managers as fairly athletic. He thought he could handle most of it, but he wasn't a strong swimmer, having only floated around in his next-door neighbor's aboveground pool a handful of times every summer. Yet he wanted to fully experience summer camp and was prepared to accept any challenge that might come his way. Or so he thought.

Devon stood up at the head of the table and asked for the boys' attention, this time tapping a spoon against a glass. It reminded Ray of a wedding reception he once attended where everyone picked up a utensil and rapped on their glasses for the bride and groom to smooch, and then everyone clapped and whooped and hollered.

"I'm not kissing in front of everyone" he promised himself when the time came.

Ray still had his pancakes to eat, but he put his fork down, looked up from his near-empty plate, and gave Devon his full attention.

"You guys are gonna' love this," he started. "I told you we had a big surprise in store, and I do mean big!

This summer, Camp Socketawaya decided to experiment with a brand new outdoor activity, and this group was chosen to give it a test run to see how it will work. Are you ready for this?"

There were a few sleepy grunts that sounded like a collective "yeah."

"Very shortly, we will be hitting the trail, but... it won't be on foot. It will be on horseback!" Devon shrieked with genuine excitement.

Judging by the wide-eyed looks on their faces, those last words got everyone's attention real fast, especially Ray's. Horseback riding was something he'd dreamed of doing since he started watching old westerns on TV, and suddenly it was about to come true. Maybe summer camp won't be so bad after all, he thought. Just then, he heard some commotion outside.

He glanced out the dining hall window and could make out a caravan of what looked like horse trailers rumbling past, headed in the direction of the trailhead. Devon dismissed the campers, shouting orders to return to the cabin, change into appropriate riding attire, and meet at the trailhead. Ray had a pair of blue jeans and a pair of hiking boots, so he put those on and looked around to see if anyone else was waiting and ready to go. There wasn't, so he slipped out and made his way to the trailhead, where the horse trailers were parked. It was a pleasant day, with a bluebird sky and bright sunshine, adding to his growing enthusiasm for his first camp activity.

He stood by and watched the handlers unload all the horses and tie them up to a nearby fencepost. He immediately had his eye on one in particular, a sturdy looking, beautifully-colored chestnut mare. Her coat was a rich, deep chocolate brown and a long, jagged white streak ran down the entire length of her nose. She was huge, with muscular legs, but seemed light on her hooves and well-behaved. Ray wanted to ride that one.

He walked over to one of the men and asked for the horse's name.

"You fancy that one, do you?" he asked, a cigarette dangling from his lips as he spoke. "Her name is Lightning 'cuz of that white streak running down her nose. It looks all jagged like a lightning bolt. You have a good eye, son. She's my favorite."

"You think I could ride her?" Ray asked. "Am I too little?"

"No, not at all. We gotta' get these horses saddled up for y'all, but I'll put in a good word and see what I can do to get you two matched up today."

Ray thanked the man and caught up with his group, which was waiting to be assigned their equine companions for the day. The owner of the horses provided some basic instruction and encouraged the boys to relax, let the horses do the work, and just enjoy the view from atop these strong, graceful creatures.

"So, let's get y'all saddled up," he said surveying the group. "Let's see, you, young man," pointing at Ray. "What's your name?"

"It's Ray, sir, actually Raymond. Raymond Fineman."

"Alright, Raymond, I believe you'd be a perfect fit for this beautiful lady right here named Lightning. Whaddya' think? Is she pretty enough for you?" he asked with a smile and a wink.

Ray smiled back, assured that the handler had kept his word and informed the owner about Ray calling dibs on her.

He was helped into the saddle, put his boots in the stirrups, took the reins in his hands, and then sat and marveled at Lightning's enormous girth and height. He leaned forward in the saddle so he could get closer to her ears and quietly introduced himself while calmly stroking her long, thick neck. He told her she was in full control, she had the reins, and he was just along for the ride and hoped they could be friends. Just then, Lightning bobbed her head up and down, let out a sharp whinny, and stomped her right front hoof. Ray was in utter disbelief at what he just witnessed, but everyone was too occupied with saddling up to notice. He was certain Lightning heard and understood his words, then communicated back to him the only way she could. That moment of bonding was something he'd treasure until his dying day.

The owner was also the group's guide for the 20-mile ride, and Ray watched him intently. He wanted to emulate the man's posture and movements, and how he communicated with his horse, both with body language and with verbal commands. The handlers called him "Chief."

Chief led the boys and their horses onto the heavily wooded trail, which was still muddy from a recent thunderstorm. The horses followed each other and walked slowly in single file, giving the boys a chance to see nature up close and from a far different perspective than they would on foot.

Ray was having the time of his life aboard Lightning. He closed his eyes and listened to the percussive sounds of the horses' hooves, making a hollow clip-clop that shattered the quiet of the wilderness but in a soothing sort of way. Together, they rode through canyons and creeks and crossed streams and open meadows. Some in the group, including

Ray, experienced scenery and surroundings they'd never seen before. They stopped for lunch on a lake shore to give the horses, and their own rear ends, a rest, and then Devon mustered them for a short hike to aid in the digestion of the franks and beans they just consumed. Otherwise, it might be a rough night in the cabin.

Ray was instantly hooked on the stillness, the sheer silence, the fresh, clean mountain air, and the breathtaking beauty he witnessed at every turn of the head. He had no idea it was always out there to be experienced, and felt a little disappointed that his parents never bothered to expose their children to it. He realized he was a nature lover, and being out in it and part of it made him feel good all over. He felt comfortable and relaxed. His mind seemed clearer. It was hard to explain, but it was as if he had suddenly plugged into some powerful energy source that wasn't there before.

The boys fed the horses carrots and sugar cubes, and then saddled up again for the 10-mile ride back to camp. Ray noticed everything looked completely different riding in the opposite direction, and he considered it yet another gift and a welcome surprise. In a subconscious way, he was learning about looking at life from different perspectives. The experience was everything he dreamed of and more.

Back at camp, the boys expressed their thanks to Chief and his crew with a rousing Camp Socketawaya cheer, and returned to the cabin to rest their weary bones before chow time. Lying on his cot, Ray rewound and replayed the entire day in his mind so he could enjoy it again while it was all still fresh.

Just when he was drifting off, the dining hall's triangular chuck wagon bell sounded, prompting a near-Pavlovian response by almost everyone to rise and proceed to the mess hall. Ray saw there were a couple of kids who were conked out and didn't hear it, but no one was waking them up. He was starved and thought they probably were too, and he didn't want them to miss a meal.

"Hey, psst! Wake up!" he said softly, giving one sleeping kid a light tap on his shoulder. "It's time for dinner."

The boy's eyes popped open, startled by Ray's wake-up call.

"Oh, OK," he said. "Guess I nodded off for a few minutes there,"

"No problem. Didn't want you to miss the meal and go hungry tonight. That would suck. Hey, I'm Ray," he said, extending his hand.

"I know. I heard you tell the Chief your name. I'm Richie. Nice to meet you, Ray."

"C'mon, let's eat. I'm starving," Ray answered.

Ray and Richie ate supper together and talked about the day they had, where they were from, what grade they were in, who their favorite baseball team was, and what they were looking forward to doing most at camp.

Once darkness fell, they concluded their first day at camp around a blazing bonfire, telling stories, singing corny songs, but best of all, scarfing down 'smores.

Ray slept like a baby that night, and during the next couple of weeks, he noticed he was sleeping better than ever before. Maybe it was the cool, mountain night air, or feeling comfortable in his surroundings, but he could feel the difference a good night's sleep made. He eagerly tried his hand at every activity that was offered, and was surprised at how proficiently he performed and how much he enjoyed taking part in each one.

Ray and Richie became close camp buddies and hung out together every day. They gradually befriended everyone in the cabin, but their friendship seemed closer than the others. Ray was grateful for his new friend and hoped they would get the chance to meet up again next summer.

In what seemed like the blink of an eye, his three-week summer camp adventure came to a bittersweet conclusion and it was pick-up day. He packed his suitcase, said his goodbyes and walked to the mess hall where his parents were waiting to take him back home.

"Boy, this was really cool!," he exclaimed with a big grin as he approached them. "It was great. I'm so glad I went. I'm so glad you let me. Did everybody miss me?"

Myrna and Sol looked at each other, broke out laughing in unison and half-jokingly told him they, too, had a nice vacation. From him. Ray wasn't sure whether he should be insulted or happy for them.

They piled into the car for the ride home to Jersey, and Ray spoke of his adventures non-stop for the entire three-hour journey. His parents told him they were glad he enjoyed himself, then reminded him that summer vacation would soon be ending, and school would be starting. It was a thought Ray didn't particularly want to entertain at that moment. School wasn't Ray's favorite subject of conversation. Yet the reality of going back was beginning to creep into his psyche, and he had to begin getting mentally prepared.

CHAPTER TWO

The Fineman's white 1960 Chevrolet Bel Air 4-door sedan's valves were knocking and it sounded throaty as it strained to climb the steep and winding road that seemed never-ending. It was hard to see clearly through the patchy early-morning fog that had settled over upstate New York's Hudson Valley.

Slumped in the driver' seat, Sol drove at a snail's pace, concentrating intently on the fog line while Myrna checked her makeup and lipstick in a tiny compact mirror, sensing their destination was near. Ray sat in the back, staring out the window and reflecting upon the life that waits for him literally around the next corner. There was dead silence in the car, but that wasn't unusual. None of them were big on talking.

A few moments later, there it was. Reality set in. Ray not only could see it, he could feel its weight.

"Welcome to Normandy Military Academy. Where Boys Become Men."

"We're here, Raymond!," Myrna shouted over her shoulder at Ray.

"Yes, mom, I can see that," Ray responded a bit sarcastically.

"Are you excited to be going back to school and seeing your classmates again?" she asked.

"Oh, I don't know, maybe one or two. Most of them are spoiled brats that come from rich families and they think they can get away with anything," he answered. "Plus, they're mean to kids who they can bully and know won't fight back."

There was no acknowledgement or reply from the front seat, only more silence, until the "Great White Whale," as Sol referred to it, lumbered up to the ivy-covered brick residence hall where Cadet Raymond Fineman would be spending the school year. They all stepped out and took a big stretch.

While Myrna grilled Ray if he packed this, that, and the other, Sol opened the trunk and pulled out Ray's two suitcases, which were loaded with everything he'd need for several months away from home since there'd be no visits in between.

"Well, son, here you go," Sol said, dropping both bags together at Ray's feet. "We have to get going. We told your Uncle Joel and Aunt Robin we'd meet them for lunch. They're taking us to the Saratoga Race Track for the day as long as we're up here."

Ray shot his mother a look of disbelief that his move-in day took a back seat to a day at the races. Again, there was awkward silence in return. No surprise; he knew his mother never objected to his father and went along with whatever he wanted to do, mostly to keep the peace. Sol was known for his hair-trigger temper and always getting his way, so she bit her tongue to avoid an ugly farewell.

"Goodbye, son. Now, behave yourself," Sol ordered. "Your mother and I don't want to have to drive all the way back here until the winter break. Promise me you'll stay out of trouble and concentrate on getting better grades, OK?"

They shook hands and Sol gave him a love tap on the cheek, a first. Ray kissed his mother goodbye, and stood solemnly watching as the Great White Whale's signature tail fins slowly disappeared. For young Raymond Fineman, life seemed nothing more than an endless series of pick-ups and drop-offs, with a smattering of family time in between. A few weeks on his winter break and a couple of months in the summer at home seemed to be plenty enough for everyone.

Ray longed to stay with his family and friends in his hometown where he could attend high school with kids from his neighborhood, and go to the movies, ride their bikes, and celebrate birthdays together. He didn't get his wish because his father decided Ray needed stricter discipline and structure in his life following his involvement in a few minor incidents involving neighborhood mischief. Rather than spending more time teaching his son those values himself, Sol instead left the heavy lifting to a military school a stone's throw away from West Point Military Academy. And as usual there wouldn't be any further discussion about it.

Ray picked up his bags and walked up two flights of stairs in search of room #207. Standing outside the door, he thought he heard someone playing a guitar. Curious, he pushed the door open and his suspicions were confirmed.

"Oh, hey! I'm Paul, but everybody back home just calls me Pea for short, as in Sweet Pea," came the distinctly southern accented voice from behind the guitar. "That's what my mama named me when I was little and it just stuck. She loved the old Popeye cartoons and Sweet Pea was Olive Oyl's baby boy. Hope you don't mind rooming with a guitar picker."

Ray was taken aback by the moment, unsure how to respond, so he let that comment slide and simply introduced himself. They made small talk while Pea continued tuning and Ray unpacked and made up his bunk. Cadets had a few remaining hours of free time that evening before classes and drills commenced the next morning, so they spent it playing ping pong and watching TV in the dormitory lounge.

It was a good ice breaker for Ray, who was fairly shy when it came to meeting people for the first time. Pea was friendly and easy-going, which made Ray feel comfortable and reduced his past anxiety about roommate assignments and compatibility. After just a few hours of knowing him, Ray was pretty sure he and Pea would get along.

Through their conversations in the ensuing weeks, Ray learned that his new roommate played quarterback on his hometown Pop Warner football team and was planning to go out for their school team. He asked Ray whether he ever played football, and when Ray told him no, Pea suggested that he should try out, too.

"I don't know, I'm not very big or strong" he said, and then quickly added, "but I am fast!"

"Well, every team needs guys who are fast," Pea said. "They can usually outrun the big fat guys. Hey, if we both make the team, you could be my wingback or flanker back."

Ray wasn't sure what those positions meant exactly, but he liked the idea of possibly playing on the same team with his new roommate. However, tackle football, wearing a helmet and pads, would be a far different ball game than the ones he occasionally played with his friends on the neighborhood ball field.

"They say I throw a nice tight spiral," Pea bragged. "Are you any good at catching passes, Ray?"

"I dunno," Ray answered. "I never had a real quarterback throw me any."

"I really need someone to practice with, throw some passes to, before the tryouts," said Pea. "Wanna' give it a try? I'd be much obliged to you."

"Sure, why not? Maybe then you can tell me if I'm good enough to try out," Ray replied.

Every afternoon for the next week or so, after finishing their classes and drills for the day, the boys headed to the empty football field. Pea taught Ray a couple of easy pass routes – a button hook and a down and out – and they'd practice it a half-dozen times. Ray was getting a heck of a workout from all of that running, and he caught most of the passes surprisingly. He quickly discovered Pea was right; he did throw a hard, tight spiral, but the ball was also much easier to catch than the wobbly wounded ducks his friends back home tossed around. And Pea saw Ray was also right when he said he was fast. He was as good, if not better, than anyone on his Pop Warner team as far as speed and the ability to run routes and catch passes. Whether physical contact would be an issue remained to be seen. Pea thought Ray was certainly good enough to try out and would have a good chance of making the team.

Tryout day arrived and the 25 or so athletes who showed up went through calisthenics and an assortment of running, passing, blocking and agility drills by a big and burly, red-headed, pear-shaped head coach named Seamus MacChesney. Everyone referred to him as Coach Mac 'n Cheese. During the entire tryouts, he never cracked a smile, and bellowed out orders, instructions, and criticisms. He busted everyone's chops for being too lazy or too slow, and was constantly blowing his whistle. That was something Ray wasn't accustomed to, and it would take some getting used to if, in fact, he made the team.

Coach Mac liked enough of what he saw in Ray to place him on the roster, and Pea was a slam-dunk selection as the team's QB. Coach Mac was impressed by his quarterbacking skills and immediately picked up on how well Ray and Pea seemed to work together, unaware of their pre-season practice sessions. The roommates continued to improve as the season progressed, and developed into a well-oiled offensive machine that dominated opponents and played a major role in the team's record seven-game winning streak.

That all came to a crashing end a few games before the end of the season when Ray caught a pass over the middle of the field and was immediately sandwiched by a pair of heavyweight linebackers. The brutal impact and his subsequent collapse to the ground broke his collarbone and gave him a concussion. He was taken to the emergency room at the local hospital for treatment and the school immediately called his parents to give them the bad news. Ray knew he'd be in trouble with his father, despite his injuries, because not only would he have to make an extra trip in the Whale before the winter break but Ray never told them he was on the football team because he knew they'd forbid it.

His parents picked him up at the hospital and they drove straight back home in near silence. Ray finished up the term recuperating at home, saving Sol several additional round trips and lessening his ire somewhat. Before he knew it, his break was over and back to school he went. Ray sat on his bunk, recounting the past few months of his recovery while Pea practiced his scales on his Martin guitar while listening to Ray and nodding his head.

Then he broke the news to Pea that his football days were over. Pea stopped playing and looked stunned.

"Wow! Did you decide that on your own, or did your parents decide for you?" he asked smiling.

"Oh, I guess it was a little of both," Ray answered. "I don't think I could go through all that again. I'm not built for it, inside and out, and I don't want to run around out there constantly worrying about getting hit."

"Coach Mac 'aint gonna like it one bit, you know," Pea warned. "He's losing one-half of his Dynamic Duo."

"I know, I know. And now I'll have to find something to fill all the spare time I'll have," Ray realized.

Pea smiled wide and played a big, fat G chord.

There was Ray's answer, right in front of him. Learn how to play something else – the guitar.

CHAPTER THREE

Pea was a fairly accomplished guitar player for a young teen, and he made his playing look so effortless that Ray wanted to give it a whirl, thinking it would be as easy as Pea made it look. He taught Ray how to finger a few simple cowboy chords and scales to get started, but within 10 minutes, he complained how much his fingers hurt. Pea explained that he had to build up calluses on his fingertips, and the only way to do that was to practice a lot. Ray realized if he wanted to pursue this new interest, he'd have to put a guitar at the top of his Hanukkah list. He could already hear his father belly aching about the noise if he ever got one.

When Ray returned to Normandy Military Academy after the winter break, he was carrying a hard-shell guitar case. Inside was a brand spanking new Martin Dreadnought six-string acoustic that he received for Hanukkah, much to his surprise and delight. Martin guitars were expensive, but also very well-made and worth the investment, so he knew his parents went way over their budget, or else got some fantastic deal, to buy it for him. He was excited, thankful, and a tad anxious, because now there was pressure for him to practice and learn how to play it. The last thing he wanted was to hear his parents ragging him about being a quitter or wasting their money on some passing fancy. Here was a golden opportunity to prove them wrong for once.

Even though he decided football was no longer his sport, Ray continued to work out with Pea, running pass routes, doing lots of push-ups and sit ups, and lifting weights. He noticed he was in the best shape of his young life, and had even grown a little bigger and stronger, which gave him a boost of confidence and self-esteem.

All of that paid off in spades when Ray was called into the Commander's office one day and informed that he earned the highest score of any Normandy cadet on the recent Marines Physical Fitness Test that was part of their physical education class every year. Ray didn't think he'd performed exceptionally well, but apparently running pass routes and doing all of those push up and sit ups with Pea were somehow worth all the sweat.

The Commander wasn't done yet, though.

"You've been selected to represent our academy, along with several others, as an example of the importance of youth focusing on physical fitness," he said. "The United States Marine Corps is filming a public service announcement in Miami, Florida, and they want you to be in it! They're offering to fly you and your family down there and put you up in a hotel for a few days while they do the filming. What do you think of that, Cadet Fineman?"

"I'm honored, Sir, but I thought there were plenty of other cadets who scored much higher than I did. I can't believe they chose me."

"They will be contacting your parents with all the details about travel and accommodations, and I'm sure you'll want to deliver this news yourself, so I suggest you call as soon as you can and give them some advance notice that the Marines will be calling."

Unsurprisingly, when his parents found out, they seemed more excited about a free trip to Miami than about congratulating Ray on his outstanding achievement and selection to represent the academy in a PSA, which by the way was making their trip possible in the first place. The travel arrangements allowed for Ray, his parents, and one other person. Since Pea was largely responsible for Ray's newfound fitness, and had become one of his closest friends, Ray chose him to accompany him and his parents on the trip.

On a cold, late February morning, the four bleary-eyed travelers departed Newark Airport for Miami, where they were picked up by a Marine Lance Corporal and driven to their hotel to await further instructions. Until then, the time was their own to do with as they wished.

They ate lunch poolside and took a swim in the hotel pool before returning to their room and finding the message light blinking on their phone. Ray was told to arrive at The Deauville Hotel at 3 pm, in dress uniform, for several hours of filming. On the short walk over from their hotel, an extraordinary event took place that would forever alter and guide the direction of Ray's life, whether he was aware of it at the time or not.

The cadets, in their crisply pressed uniforms and highly-buffed shoes, were walking briskly, nervously, energetically, a fair distance ahead of Ray's parents. An elderly couple approached them out of the blue.

"Excuse me boys, we're staying at the Deauville Hotel, and they gave us a couple of tickets to some rock and roll music show here tonight that we have no interest in attending. We were wondering if you'd be interested in having them?" said the lady. "It says here on the tickets it's somebody called the Beatles. You look like such nice wholesome boys, all sharply dressed in your military uniforms, we thought you might enjoy it."

Ray heard of The Beatles from his older brother, Simon, and older sister, Bonnie Lee, but he didn't know anything about them or their music. The boys graciously accepted the couples' thoughtful gift and thanked them, then turned to Ray's parents and asked for permission to go after they were finished with the filming.

"C'mon, Pops," Ray pleaded. "We're old enough to go by ourselves. We're 14 going on 15 years old. You can trust us to stay out of trouble. We both like music, plus we'll be in uniform, so we have to be on our best behavior. They always tell us at the academy, you never know who may be watching."

Sol must have been in a good mood because he agreed without much convincing. They went to the filming, where there were about 50 other boys and girls their age congregating in the hotel lobby. Ray asked around and found out that some producer calls your name, you go into a room with lights and a camera, they ask you a few questions, and then you read a script a few times. Before long, Ray's name was called and he sprung to his feet, smiled wide at the producer lady, and went in and delivered what he considered only a mediocre performance at best. He showed he was no actor, but he could tell they liked him and the fact he looked sharp in his uniform. They told him it greatly improved his chances of making the final cut.

They all went out to dinner afterward to celebrate and Ray heard his father say for the first time out loud that he was proud of him. That was as satisfying as the meal itself.

His parents went back to their hotel, and it was time for Ray and Pea to return to the Deauville Hotel for what was billed as the "really big show." When they arrived, they were directed to a large ballroom that had a makeshift stage and humongous banks of PA speakers and lighting trusses, but most notably, several television cameras. The Beatles were set to perform on The Ed Sullivan Show, a weekly variety program featuring a range of celebrity and novelty acts that typically broadcast from New York City and The Ed Sullivan Theater. The Beatles were on a nationwide tour and staying in Miami, so it was decided to break from tradition and do the show from there. Ray and Pea didn't know it, but they were about to witness rock and roll history and become two members of a very small group of people who attended that live show. The size of the audience was estimated at 300 tops.

What a historic show it was. From the second the Fab Four, as they were fast becoming known, was introduced and Sullivan barely finished introducing the band by name, it was volume 10, ear-shattering, non-stop screeching and wailing from adoring teenage girls in the audience. They flailed their arms, shouted out the name of their favorite Beatle – John, Paul, George or Ringo, and some even fainted. Ray and Pea looked at each other in total shock and disbelief. Even though they could barely hear the music over the cacophony coming from the audience, they couldn't help notice the effect it had on the young ladies in particular.

The Beatles played "She Loves You" and "I Wanna Hold Your Hand," two hit songs that were at the top of the music charts and receiving non-stop airplay on the radio. The boys had never seen a live show, so they didn't have any means of comparison to this one. But as two teenagers who liked music and were beginning to show an interest in girls, they both thought "hey, maybe someday we could do that, too."

Subconsciously, a seed was sown that evening that would eventually sprout and become Ray's tree of life. That seed was singing, playing music, and performing for an audience, and as it grew and matured, it gave him roots, sustenance and nourishment, both physically and spiritually.

When they returned to Normandy Military Academy after the trip to Miami, Ray was consumed with playing his guitar. He stopped working out with Pea and chose to practice instead, sometimes playing six hours a day. He wanted to get good in a hurry so he could start or join a band. However, all of that playing left little time for focusing on his schoolwork, and his grades were suffering badly. He finished out the year with his worst academic performance ever and was told that because he failed to meet the school's academic standards, he wasn't welcome to return in the fall.

That entire summer, Ray stayed in his room and practiced all day. He grew his hair long and styled it similar to the Beatles, which became a bone of contention especially with his father. Finally, Sol had enough and issued Ray an ultimatum: either get a haircut and a job, or get out of his house until he did.

The next day, Ray bid farewell to his family, hopped on a bus to the Port Authority Terminal in New York City, and headed downtown to Greenwich Village. He heard there were a lot of clubs and musicians there and thought he might meet people who could help him get started in the music business.

He slept on a park bench the first night, if it could even be called sleep. He basically kept one eye open all night to make sure nobody would rob him or, heaven forbid, steal his guitar. That instrument was going to be his bread and butter, and he'd fight to the death to defend against anyone trying to take it.

At daybreak, he packed up and started walking around the park in search of a public restroom. It began to dawn on him that life on the street was going to be full of challenges like washing up and using the facilities, so he had to focus on getting a roof over his head, someway, somehow.

In the distance he heard what sounded like someone singing and followed it to an open space where a guy with a trashed guitar was slamming the strings and caterwauling gibberish. Ray noticed the guy's guitar case was close by and there was money in it. Bingo!

Ray knew he could sing and play better than that so-called street musician, so he found his own spot, unpacked his guitar, and in that moment, realized what it was like to be a busker. He loved singing and playing for passersby and seeing the enjoyment on their faces. The tips were barely enough to keep him fed, or to afford a room at the YMCA. He slept in shelters occasionally, but never felt safe. It was easy to get robbed or injured, and Ray wanted no part of that.

Fairly diligent about showing up most days, he became a familiar sight to the locals who lived in the area. One of those was a musician named Adam Yablonski who regularly saw and heard him perform. Out of the blue, he asked Ray if he would be interested in auditioning for a band he was putting together called Gulliver. He desperately needed a guitarist and thought Ray might fit the bill.

He got the job and after a few months of rehearsals, the band landed a steady gig in the Village playing what was billed as The Crotch Watchers Matinee at a place called Cafe Wha? It was a well-known neighborhood bar and nightclub, featuring live music and topless dancers. Ray, who'd now earned the nickname "Windy" for his long and winding storytelling style, was in his element and couldn't believe how quickly his luck was turning.

It seemed like everything was moving at warp speed. All of a sudden, he befriended people like the great Big Band drummer, Gene Krupa, who was a fixture at the club every afternoon enjoying the matinee. He said it was a warm-up for his performance later in the evening with his big band.

Ray met world-renowned jazz trumpet player Miles Davis and became close friends and eventually roommates with his son, Miles, Jr. Drugs and booze were everywhere for anyone interested, and Ray usually was.

It was a time of free love and the onset of the sexual revolution; of experimentation and experiencing the best and most of every aspect of life. On one of those occasions, Ray was introduced to a stunningly attractive Lithauanian-born jazz dancer named Silka, and he was instantly infatuated with her beauty and quirky sense of humor. It didn't take long for that crush to evolve into a deep and abounding love that soon led to a monogamous relationship.

Ray knew he found his soul mate when she asked him to move in with her. He had steady work, so he could pay some of the rent, but most importantly, they could be together all the time. He played local clubs and did some recording with Gulliver, who were beginning to create some music industry buzz as up-and-comers to watch.

The band hired an agent and soon after, they were scheduled to tour through the south and up and down the eastern seaboard for several months. Ray was over the moon with excitement; it was a dream come true. At the same time, he was crestfallen knowing he was soon to be temporarily separated from the new love of his life.

CHAPTER FOUR

"Windy" acclimated to touring and life on the road in no time. Gulliver was roaring up and down the east coast, playing mostly in bars and clubs, and a few county fairs in between, drawing decent crowds and warmer than expected receptions. The band was getting tighter every day, both as musicians and as band mates.

Ray was missing Silka badly but always remained faithful to his pledge of monogamy. There were many opportunities to stray, and the temptation was strong and ever-present, but he was a man of his word, and when he made a promise, it was in the vault, a done deal.

Silka missed Ray terribly, too. On some of their near nightly phone calls, she'd casually question his fidelity, and then count the days until his return. Ray often wondered if she was honoring their arrangement as he was, trying to think of who might make a move to steal her away while he was temporarily out of the picture. They didn't have a lot of male friends, so it could be Dieter or Serge from the dance troupe who she talks a lot about. Or the doorman who always gives her a wink when they leave but doesn't acknowledge him. Or the young guy at the deli where they buy their sandwiches on the weekends. Christ, it could be anyone, he thought. She's gorgeous, talented, and kind-hearted. Who wouldn't desire a woman like that?

The band was just beginning the southern leg of the tour, working their way west out of the Florida panhandle on their way to New Orleans. The boys were starting to show signs of exhaustion from the grind of the road, the liquor and late nights, and any substance in which they cared to indulge. There were a half-dozen dates remaining on their tour schedule and they knew they just had to suck it up.

Windy was half-asleep in his seat as their tour bus rolled into the town of Clarksville, Kentucky and pulled up in front of an old movie theater. He was trying to make out the letters through squinty eyes and guessed that it said Stanley. He wasn't certain because several of the letters weren't lit.

Everyone was suddenly energized by the thought of playing a venue other than a nasty bar or a seedy club where their music wasn't always appreciated. Here, they were presented with a huge stage, outstanding acoustics, quality sound, and the icing on the cake: dressing rooms. They considered it a welcome step up in their status as a touring band to be offered such a luxury at this stage of their existence. They were relatively new on the scene, and like anything new and different, were making noise and generating some chatter among industry execs. There were rumors floating around that one of the major labels was interested in signing them to a record deal.

The band never sounded better that night. They played their asses off and absolutely killed it, and the calls and whistles for an encore proved it. They never had one of those before, either. The performance may have given them the shot of adrenaline they needed to wake up and carry them through the remaining gigs.

Windy was backstage after the show chatting with a few fans who caught the band's last show, when two guys approached him and asked if they could speak privately. He didn't know who they were or what it was about, but they looked like undercover police officers that he'd seen on TV, so he excused himself and agreed to talk to them.

"Am I in some kind of trouble?" he asked anxiously. He did a quick scan of his brain for anything he might have done recently that could be considered even remotely criminal.

"No, no, nothing like that," one of them replied. "We work in research and development for the US Army and since you look like a pretty cool guy, we were wondering if you wanted to be part of an experiment we're doing."

"Really? What kind of experiment are we talking about?," Ray asked.

"We think it might be right up your alley. It's a clinical drug trial for LSD and we're studying how it might be used as a weapon of war. We're experimenting with the right dosage that will disorient the enemy."

"That sounds pretty cool. I haven't tripped in awhile so yeah, I might be interested. What do I have to do?" Ray wondered.

"Just open wide," one of them replied.

"Right here? Now? Are you guys crazy?"

"It'll take just a second. No one's looking."

Windy surveyed the backstage area and didn't see anyone. He turned back and did as they said. One of them had an eyedropper and squeezed out two drops on Ray's tongue. It tasted a little funky, so he washed it down with a swig of beer.

"You're off to see the wizard now," one said with a big smile. "Just follow that yellow brick road. We want to keep an eye on you and monitor your behavior for the next few hours back at our lab. You got some time. It's just down the road."

It was still fairly early and Ray was a bit of a night owl, so he agreed on the condition that they return him when they promised. He had to be sure he got on that bus before it pulled out at daybreak. As they walked out to the guy's car, Ray was starting to get hit.

"Whoa, this is coming on strong," he grinned. "Amazing already. I can't feel my feet! There's this incredible wave of energy working its way up through my body. What an amazing rush!"

Once at the lab on base, the two men asked Ray basic questions to observe how he processed thoughts. They asked him to draw shapes and figures, and tested his reflexes and reactions, as a way to measure his hand-eye coordination. He could barely respond through his non-stop laughing and inability to remember questions. He couldn't focus and displayed the attention span of a three year-old.

Within a couple of hours, the men got what they needed and Ray was well into a lollapalooza of an acid trip. As the Army's guinea pig, he just sampled the purest form known to man of lysergic diethylamide, or LSD 25, and before it was turned into a chemical weapon of war. The effects of it tested his limits and he felt as if he was losing control. He'd never reached this level of nirvana before and had to concentrate on getting a grip, or wind up in the emergency room. That would never fly with the group.

The men dropped Ray off in the parking lot of a hotel where the bus was parked overnight, exchanged phone numbers, and said their goodbyes. It was a little after 2 am when Ray climbed aboard the bus and announced his return, expecting them to be pleased. They weren't. They'd been asleep.

As high as he was, it never dawned on him that he could be disturbing his band mates' slumber.

"God dammit, Windy, we're trying to get some sleep here and you're just raging. Where the hell did you go? We were looking all over for you," Adam barked.

"Long story. Too late. Tell you tomorrow."

He climbed into his sleeping compartment, pulled the privacy curtain, and tried to close his eyes and lie still, but he was freaked out by the brightly colored kaleidoscopic images that morphed into giant horned toads and disfigured, fire-breathing dinosaurs. He heard his heart pounding in his chest, and imagined his lungs filling and emptying with every breath. He was burning hot and sweating profusely, and minutes later, he was freezing cold and shivering. He took a few hits on his hash pipe, got up and paced the length of the bus the rest of the night, mumbling nonsense and feeling outside of himself. He calmed down enough to try to get some sleep, and wound up nodding off for an hour or so.

On the next gig, the boys in the band noticed there was something different about Windy. He wasn't his usual long-winded, storytelling, conversation-occupying self. He wasn't smiling, and he seemed to go in and out of a fog, fairly lucid and in the moment, and then in a haze, and part of another world on another planet. He looked pre-occupied or worried about something. But most importantly, he started playing the wrong chords, mixing up songs, singing off-key, and forgetting lyrics. A band on the brink of actually making it can't suffer that.

Adam approached him after another mistake-laden show and asked him directly if he was OK, and if anything was wrong. Was he missing Silka? Plain burned out from the tour? Partying and burning the candle at both ends?

"You seemed different after that Clarksville show," said Adam. "You came back to the bus very late and woke us up. You couldn't stand still and it was like you were speaking in tongues. Did you find some good speed or something?"

"I think so. I really don't remember. I must have really tripped out that night," Ray answered. "It was weird, like my brain suddenly became an Etch-a-Sketch and somebody came along, shook it, and everything vanished. The screen was blank for a few days, but I'm starting to put some of the pieces back together."

"Well, we're worried about you, man. If there's something wrong, we have to know so we can try to fix it," Adam told him.

"I'd tell you if there was," Ray replied. "I'm sorry. I know my head hasn't been entirely in the game, and I really don't know why. Don't worry. I'll be alright."

"Hope so, Windy. You know the band has a lot riding on these last shows. We need you to be solid with your singing and playing. Think back to those busking days."

Even after the talk, Ray looked distant on stage, and his voice and rhythm guitar playing sounded shaky and tentative, which it never did before. He acted aloof and didn't engage with his bandmates, and that was odd. He was always very active and animated while performing. Truth be told, he was a ham.

Things came to a head following a show in Biloxi, Mississippi after Ray checked out mentally and stopped playing. He looked paralyzed and appeared like he didn't know where he was. He didn't seem to realize it was a live show with a live audience.

After the show, Adam noticed that Ray had his head down, didn't speak to anybody, and looked sullen. He asked Ray if he wanted to grab a cup of coffee or something to eat and unwind. He thought a nice walk and some fresh air would do them both good.

Adam and Ray found a late-night diner still open a few blocks away, and ordered up burgers and french fries with chocolate milk shakes. Adam made small talk as Ray devoured his meal and said little.

Waiting for the check, Adam cleared his throat and stared at Ray.

"Windy, I have a confession to make. I asked you to come here because I wanted to tell you privately that the band decided you needed to go or else we'd risk losing our chance to finally make it big."

Ray looked at him blankly and didn't speak a word. Adam didn't know if he was just gobsmacked or in one of his trances.

"I wanted you to have a good meal to fill you up before I give you this," Adam said, handing him an envelope.

Ray opened it and found a one-way bus ticket to New York City, and three $100 bills.

"We want you to go back home, get some rest and relax, be with Silka, and get yourself right," Adam told him. "There's a few hundred bucks there to help get you on your feet, and we'll ship all your belongings and gear so you'll have it in a couple of days.

"I really hated to do this, man, and I hope you can understand that each of us has to be at the top of our game, every night. We can't half-step it, and that's what you're doing. We all know you're better than this and you can be again. We've seen and heard you play at a professional level. But you 'aint doing that now, and we thought being home would help you get your head right."

Looking down at the floor, Ray said, "You're right. I haven't been myself lately and I can't let that stand in the way of the band's success. I have to figure it out somehow. Lifting his head up, he continued. "I'm sorry I let you down, Adam. But I want you to know how much I appreciated you giving me a chance. And I hope I can work my way back into the band's good graces some day."

"Let's try to make that happen, man. You can do it."

The bus to New York was due to arrive at the terminal shortly, so they shook hands, said their goodbyes, and bear-hugged each other with tears welling in their eyes. Turning away, each wondered if this was, in fact, the end of the road for Ray.

CHAPTER FIVE

The scenery rushed by and appeared nothing more than a blur through the filthy, palm-smudged window that made everything outside look cloudy and shapeless. The view seemed a fitting metaphor for Ray's brain at the moment. Bits and pieces of the past few months were slowly beginning to emerge, but what he was able to recall was still fuzzy and out of focus at best.

The painfully long bus ride back to the city gave Ray the opportunity to finally settle down, and use the time to try and clear his head so he could process the events that led to his departure from the band. He knew he let the people closest to him down, especially Adam, who gave him the chance to graduate from the street and make it to the stage as a touring musician in a band with some promise.

Slouched down in his seat and watching the outside world fly by reminded Ray of those long days riding on the band bus, and the tight bonds that formed where his bandmates became almost like brothers to him in a very short period of time. The memory put a faint smile on his face. He missed those boys badly and wondered if they missed him.

With hours upon hours to go, and little to do but sit and think, Ray began connecting the dots and realized that the tiny dose of pure lysergic acid diethylamide LSD25 that an Army researcher gave him after one of the shows was probably to blame for his mental breakdown and subsequent firing. Still under its powerful effects for days and weeks afterward prevented him from noticing his sudden inability to recall, think logically, and interact socially. He wasn't even able to carry on a simple conversation because he couldn't conjure up the thoughts and words.

The constant drone inside the bus was strangely hypnotic, sending Ray into a mild trance where he soon succumbed to the tidal wave of physical and mental fatigue he'd been suppressing for so long. He was thoroughly exhausted from all the energy he devoted trying to convince everyone he was fine and functioning normally, when it was clear to everyone else that he wasn't. When all was said and done, the only person he ended up fooling was himself.

The bus made a few brief pit stops at stations that were usually located in the seediest part of town, so to be on the safe side, Ray remained in his seat. The last thing he needed was to walk off, forget where he was, and get rolled for the little cash he had on him.

The next 12 hours were pure torture, but Ray passed them with pleasant thoughts of Silka and imagining their long-awaited reunion. Seeing her again was the only silver lining in this dark cloud hanging over his head. He couldn't wait to hold her in his arms, feel her warmth and her loving embrace again, hear that funny little giggle when he said or did something weird, to lie in bed beside her and simply be awestruck at the indescribable beauty of her toned and sculpted body. In Ray's eyes, God broke the mold after creating Silka. She was practically perfect, and there could only be one like her. Truly, she was a rare gem.

No one had ever loved Ray like Silka did. He never dreamed it was even possible that a woman could love a man that much. When they were together, it was the moon and the stars and, in a word, heavenly. Ray made it a point to thank God every day for their paths crossing, becoming fast friends, and falling so deeply in love. They believed they were destined to be true soul mates, and he considered her a once-in-a-lifetime gift and a blessing from above. The Hand of Fate rested squarely on his shoulder.

Deep in his thoughts about Silka, Ray barely noticed that dawn was breaking and the sun was just rising over the Manhattan skyline, meaning he was almost home. After months on the road and desperately missing her, he was so anxious at the thought of finally being together again that he started hyperventilating. He'd never experienced that before. But tucked away in the far recesses of his mind was a haunting fear his anxiety would trigger a flashback, or cause him to forget what he was doing or where he was going. He knew he had to get a hold of himself and relax.

The bus exited the Lincoln Tunnel and corkscrewed up the Port Authority's ramps all the way to the top, and parked in a stall to unload the passengers. There were hundreds of other buses, all with their engines running, spewing diesel fumes and fouling the air. Ray stayed in his seat and waited for all the passengers to leave before making his exit. He slowly regained his composure and walked out into the busy Port terminal, which was an all-out visual assault with its bright lights and everyone moving about at breakneck speed. He would have to readjust his motor and give it a major tune-up to keep up with the speed and chaos he'd soon be facing every day in New York City.

He caught an escalator down to street level and exited onto 8th Avenue and 43rd Street, with the familiar aroma of Sabrett's gutter dogs and burnt chestnuts in the air. As tired as he was, the buzz of the city energized him and he decided to walk the 20 or so blocks to their apartment in the Chelsea district of Manhattan. It was a glorious day and Ray still needed time to compose himself and prepare for the moment he'd been waiting for all these months. He looked like 10 cents worth of God help us from wearing the same dirty clothes for a couple of days riding on the bus and he desperately needed a shower and shave. It was hardly the way he planned to present himself, but he was counting on sweet-natured Silka to understand the unusual circumstances leading to his present appearance.

They lived in a high-rise apartment building on W. 23rd Street in a cozy love nest that measured a scant 500 square feet. It was small, but still manageable for two respectful and considerate adults who always enjoyed each other's company and spent a lot of time together.

Ray pulled open the big glass door to the building and walked through the lobby to an open elevator. He could feel his heart pounding and his stomach was tied up in knots. It was the same feeling he had on his first date with Silka – nervous, excited, and low on self-esteem and confidence. He punched the button for the 7th floor, the doors closed, and as each floor light lit up, he silently prayed for God's blessing that he and Daina could just pick up where they left off. Exiting the elevator, he walked down the hall to #777 and stood there for a moment to take a deep breath. He lost his keys somewhere along the tour so he wasn't able to quietly unlock the door, then barge in and yell "Surprise!" When he raised his hand to knock on the door, it suddenly opened, and there she was, like double cherry pie. A vision of loveliness. Dingy white T-shirt underneath dirty overalls, hair piled up in a bun, no make up, wearing

Playtex Living gloves, and holding a trash bag in one hand. What a sight it was to behold.

"Raymond! Oh, my God! You made it!"

Silka called him Raymond when she was very intense or serious. "Welcome home, sweetie pie. I've been so worried about you."

She ripped off her gloves and reached out, grabbed his smiling face with both her hands and laid a long, passionate kiss on him right there in the hallway. It'd been ages since he tasted those tender lips, and all he kept thinking was, 'I'm home sweet home.'

Typically, it was Ray's chore to take out the trash, and he offered it as his first chore back, but Silka suggested he come with, so their first order of business was a trip to the trash chute. That definitely was not the first thing Ray had on his mind when he got home.

Back in the apartment, they showered and got changed. Ray only had the clothes on his back to wear and his belongings wouldn't be arriving for a day or two. He found a pair of sweatpants and a t-shirt to change into and Silka matched him. They weren't planning on going anywhere and just wanted to be comfy cozy.

Sitting on the couch sharing a bottle of red wine and listening to some Beatles music, Ray pulled the money envelope out of his pocket, opened it up, and gleefully removed one of the two joints Adam slipped in at the last minute to help him stay mellow for his trip. He wanted to save them for a moment like this. After a few hits, they were feeling nicely buzzed and, kicking back with a glass of wine, just took a deep breath and savored the moment together. Awash in euphoria, all was right in their world.

They filled each other in on the things they did to keep their minds occupied during that stretch of separation; how they endured the incessant pangs of abstinence; and what they thought about monogamy after they had a taste of it. They agreed it would have been a piece of cake to cheat on each other, but deep down, they really wanted to put their love and their trust in one another to the ultimate test.

Then the conversation turned to work, and instantly Ray felt a certain uneasiness in his gut about what was to follow. It was inevitable Silka would want to hear the full story, with every detail he could recall. She spoke briefly on the phone with Adam a few days ago, who called to tell her only that Ray left the tour, was on a bus home, and would be arriving in a day or two. He offered no explanation other than saying he preferred that Ray do the explaining.

"So what happened, Raymond? Adam didn't say much. He wanted you to tell me," Silka said.

He lowered his head for a few seconds, and then looked her straight in the eye.

"Well, I hate to admit it, but I'm not entirely sure of every little thing that may have occurred for a few days after I took this really pure acid after a show. These Army guys made it seem like it would be a patriotic thing to do, and I'd be contributing to science and research. So, in the moment, I stupidly agreed. I had no idea it was so pure and could do that much damage."

Silka sat silently, staring blankly at the living room wall and trying to process what he just said.

"Bad decision, Raymond," she sighed, shaking her head. Her quiet sigh was followed seconds later by an uncharacteristically explosive outburst.

"Why in the world would you do something crazy like that? Taking acid from two guys you didn't know? What if you're permanently brain damaged now? What happens if we want to have children? Will their brains be scrambled, too?"

Ray didn't know exactly how to answer those questions, which came at him like machine gun fire. Gathering his thoughts, he asked if she would please calm down so he could explain his side of the story. She owed him that courtesy at least.

"You might be jumping to conclusions a little soon here, darlin'," he said calmly. "Yeah, looking back now it seems like a dumb thing to do. I've done my share of acid, and I just assumed it would be like that, no problem. I never experienced anything near that level before. It was so intense and seemed to go forever. "

"Who are these Army guys? Have they been in contact with you at all?" Silka asked.

"They gave me a business card and it should be in with the stuff they're shipping," he began. "Should be here in a day or two."

Silka cut him off.

"They gotta' know what happened, and the damage it has done to you," she pleaded. "And how to fix it if it needs fixing. What was it you were being used as a guinea pig for?"

Ray replied, "That's an interesting way to put it, but I really can't argue with you there. The guy told me the Army was studying whether LSD could be used as a chemical weapon of war. I just felt I couldn't say no to him."

The temperature in the room suddenly dropped, so Ray put his arm around Silka and pulled her close to him.

"I think you know how much I adore you, Silka, and I would never do anything that would harm you, me, or us, intentionally. In hindsight it was a huge mistake, and I'd never make it again, and I hope you'll forgive my sorry ass."

She looked into Ray's droopy Basset-hound eyes, and managed a sliver of a grin while shaking her head; half of her pissed off, the other half sort of understanding, but not enough to give him a full pass. She moved even closer and laid her head on his shoulder.

Within a few minutes, they were both passed out on the couch from a combination of the wine, weed, and a heavy dose of pure bliss. At least that's what Ray surmised when he finally awoke around dawn and saw he was alone on the couch. Silka came into the living room after showering and explained she wanted him to sleep after his long trip and didn't want to disturb him.

"I wouldn't have minded," he shot back. "So instead of you, I wind up with an aching back and a stiff neck."

"We'll have to work on that later," she said playfully, returning to the bedroom to get ready for a rehearsal.

A quick smoothie and a good-bye kiss later, there Ray was, alone on the couch, just sitting and thinking. He had so much going on in his mind, and so much he was trying to retrieve at the same time, and that jumble of thoughts were like atoms colliding. He had no clothes, no shoes, no guitar, no shave kit, but he did have some money and one joint left. He wondered who might still be around who could help him in that department, too.

It was a gray day, and seemed to drag on forever. Ray was tempted to spark that jay to get himself right, but decided to wait until Silka got home.

Right around the time she was expected home, the phone rang and Ray quickly answered.

"Hey Sugar, that you? Coming home soon? We have some unfinished business to tend to ya' know," he teased.

"Actually, I'm afraid I won't be coming home tonight, Ray. I just found out my mother had a stroke today, and I have to be with her, so I'm spending the night at her apartment in Brooklyn. I'm so sorry."

So was Ray and he offered his sympathy. But in his gut, he sensed there was something in the tone of Silka's voice that didn't sound quite right.

CHAPTER SIX

As daylight was breaking, Ray finally closed his eyes and drifted off to sleep on the living room couch. He had been up all night wracking his brain about Silka and the lingering effects of his experimental LSD trip. He was hopeful she would be patient with him and understand that in hindsight, it was something he should have thought through before he did it, and in the end regretted it. He prayed for her forgiveness, and for them to resume their happy lives together once things settled down. There seemed to be a lot of commotion in both their lives at the moment.

The phone rang and shook Ray out of his semi-slumber. The clock on the wall said 6:20. He thought it might be Silka calling to say good morning and telling him she'd be home in time for dinner. He sprung from the couch and rushed to the phone.

"Good morning, is that you sugar," he said with a wry grin.

A gruff voice responded, "Sugar?". Since when do you call your father sugar?"

"Oh my God, Dad, I'm sorry. I thought it was Silka. Is something wrong?"

His father proceeded to tell him that his brother Simon was in the hospital and may have broken his neck diving into a shallow pool at a neighbor's pool party. He wanted Ray to know in case he wanted to visit them and see his brother. Ray could barely catch his breath long enough to answer he'd be there as soon as he could. He hung up the phone and stood there stunned, trying to process what he just heard. A thousand images swirled in his head, but he knew he had to keep it together mentally and make a plan to be there with his family.

He didn't know how to get in touch with Silka since she called from a pay phone somewhere in Brooklyn, nor did he know where her mother lived so he could get her number. He left a note on the kitchen counter explaining the emergency visit to New Jersey with the promise he would return as soon as he possibly could. And that he loved her very much and couldn't wait to see her.

He packed up some clothes and toiletries into a knapsack, grabbed a few pieces of fresh fruit, and left on a half-hour walk to the Port Authority Terminal to catch a bus back home to New Jersey. His mind was cluttered, and he dreaded the thought of this latest anxiety triggering one of those awful flashback episodes.

The Port Authority terminal was chaotic and bustling as usual, but nothing Ray hadn't seen before. He purchased his ticket on the main concourse and navigated his way up a couple of escalators to the terminal floor where his bus was waiting. He climbed aboard and off they went through the side streets on the west side of Manhattan and into the cavernous, mile-long endurance test called the Lincoln Tunnel. Two narrow lanes of high-speed traffic, ultra-bright lights, dingy tiled walls, and loaded with the noxious fumes from the exhaust pipes of a million vehicles passing through every day. Ray eased back in his seat, closed his eyes and tried to relax, but he was still jumpy.

An hour later the bus rolled into the Kenilworth bus terminal where Myrna and Sol were waiting to pick him up and then go to the hospital together. They hugged and kissed each other hello, and tried to put on happy faces, but there was noticeable tension and uneasiness in the air.

The ride to the hospital was somber and didn't offer much information about Simon's condition or prognosis. Ray knew that a broken neck often resulted in paralysis, but he didn't want to get too far ahead of himself and think worst case scenario. Better to go with an optimistic mindset instead.

When they walked into Simon's room in the hospital and saw all the cords and tubes and monitors attached to him they were taken aback. Myrna gasped and began tearing up. Ray locked arms with her and they slowly approached the bed. Simon was sedated and resting, wearing a special neck splint, awaiting a neurosurgeon's visit. There wasn't much they could do at the moment, so they decided to return the next day. Ray reached out and took Simon's hand, and gave it a gentle squeeze.

He whispered, "I got you, brother man. I'm right here by your side and always will be. Now don't you stop fightin', ya' hear me?"

Ray swore he felt Simon squeeze his hand ever so slightly in reply, and that gave Ray a glimmer of hope.

The entire family visited the next day and found Simon awake and able to converse a little. Although he was mildly sedated, he managed a hint of a smile and Ray could tell he was happy to see everyone. The seriousness of the accident and the potential impact it would have on their lives was just beginning to set in, but now wasn't the time to bring it up. Simon was alive, feeling no pain, resting comfortably, and getting round-the-clock care, so for the moment that was their focus. In the back of everyone's mind, however, lingered dreaded thoughts of Simon paralyzed and living out his life as a paraplegic or quadraplegic. They hated to think the worst, but it was hard to ignore the very real possibility. They'd just have to wait for word from his doctor for a diagnosis and course of treatment.

Simon was nodding off and talking gibberish so it was time to go. They kissed his head and wished him sweet dreams, promising to see him tomorrow. They barely spoke on the ride home, each deeply pensive and preoccupied by the suddenness and intensity of this tragic mishap besetting their family. After arriving home, Ray told them he was too keyed up to go inside and was going to take a walk around the neighborhood to help settle him down.

The stroll around the block resurrected fond memories of him and his brother racing each other home from school, riding their bikes up and down these streets, playing baseball and football on those fields, and swimming all day in their best friend's pool. As they got older, the brothers would often go hiking and cross-country skiing together and shared a deep appreciation for the wonders of nature. Ray was trying to imagine what Simon's life might look like now.

Ray's thought process was interrupted by the faint sound of bells chiming in the distance. He recognized that tone immediately. It was the sound of the Good Humor man letting all the kids in the neighborhood know it was time for ice cream. The truck would lazily cruise up and down the quiet, tree-lined streets and wait for someone to run out of the house and scream "Stop!" And the truck actually would.

The truck turned slowly onto the Fineman's street and Ray could see the driver gently tugging on the rope that was attached to four bells that announced his presence, but he didn't notice children heading toward the truck. The driver made his way up the street and was rolling past when Ray suddenly stopped walking and signaled the driver to pull over and stop. Ray thought to himself, "I could use a little good humor right now."

The driver greeted him with a big smile and asked what he was in the mood for today. Ray perused the menu on the side of the truck and noticed a few items he used to order. It was usually either an ice cream sandwich or a strawberry shortcake popsicle. Today, he decided to go with the ice cream sandwich.

As he was unwrapping it, the driver asked if he lived in the area. He responded he was visiting his folks and this was the street where he grew up. He was just taking a walk and seeing the trademark white truck and hearing those bells brought back a flood of childhood memories.

The driver grinned and introduced himself as Giacomo. They exchanged pleasantries and Ray thanked him and turned back toward the sidewalk. Giacomo blurted out, "Hey, Ray, if you know anybody who wants to make some easy money driving one of these trucks for a week, let me know. I have some out-of-town business I have to tend to and need to take a week off. I need someone I can trust to fill in for me. Hey, what about you? You look like someone I can trust."

Ray laughed and thanked him, but told him he lived in the city now and didn't know anybody around the neighborhood who'd be interested in his offer. Plus, he never drove a truck and didn't have a license anyway. Then, like a lightning bolt striking, it dawned on him that he was running out of money and was planning on staying with his parents for another week or so. He had no way of reaching Silka; they hadn't spoken since he left. But here was a short-term gig, getting paid cash under the table, and the work is about as easy as it gets. What could be so hard about driving around and selling ice cream, he thought to himself. And it's only for a week.

They talked it over some more and agreed on $500 pay for the week, working a few hours a day covering the streets in his old neighborhood. Ray thought it might prove to be a nice distraction from the current family crisis, and he would still be able to visit his brother in his spare time.

They shook hands and then Giacomo looked at Ray and, in a whisper, asked him whether he indulged. Ray assumed he was referring to smoking weed, and he smiled and nodded his head yes.

"I knew it! I can always read people and figure who's cool and who ain't. After talking to you for five minutes I knew you're cool," Giacomo said. "I'll make sure you're well taken care of in that department, too since you're doing me this favor."

Three days later, following incessant shaming from his parents when they learned of his newfound employment, Ray reported to the garage where the ice cream trucks were loaded and dispatched. He met with Giacomo briefly before beginning his evening shift.

"I really appreciate you helping me out, Ray," Giacomo told him. "Just have fun and seriously, don't work too hard. I'll ride along with you for a while and then turn you loose and let you solo."

On the way to Ray's old neighborhood, Giacomo instructed him to slow down and up ahead turn into Riccardo's Pasta House. He explained he gives the owner a deal on Italian ices and has to make a quick delivery. Ray nodded and immediately, out of the corner of his eye, saw a large man wearing an apron approach the truck. Ray turned to inform Giacomo, who was busy lifting a large cardboard box out of the truck's freezer.

"Here Ray, can you hand this to him?"

Ray thought it was odd that Giacomo didn't meet the man, but he took the box and stepped out of the truck.

Instantly, the entire parking lot lit up with half a dozen police cars, and cops pointing guns, screaming orders for everybody to show their hands. Ray couldn't figure out what the heck was happening but he knew it couldn't be good. They were ordered to turn around and put their hands behind their back. They were handcuffed and placed under arrest for marijuana possession and distribution. Apparently, Giacomo was dealing serious weight out of the Good Humor truck and had been under surveillance for several weeks. Ray's new job started and ended with a drug bust.

Despite Ray strenuously protesting, and Giacomo's insistence that Ray had nothing to do with it and was unaware of the contraband, the cops hauled them in and placed them in a holding cell until they could find a judge for an arraignment. They spent four long hours in the slam before they were paraded in front of a cranky, half-asleep old coot who wasn't exactly thrilled about being rousted out of bed in the middle of the night. He was in a foul mood and wanted this over and done with quickly.

Looking at Giacomo and his partner in crime, he said, "You two knuckleheads are hereby remanded to jail to await trial for intent to distribute, and you, Mr. Good Humor Man, I'm not entirely convinced you were involved in this dirty deal, but you were there and it's also possible you knew about it. Then again, maybe you were just a clueless stooge. So I'm giving you a choice. You can go to prison with them and do who knows how much time, or I can place you in a drug rehabilitation program called Odyssey House. It's a chance to help you get your life straightened out. So, what'll it be?"

Ray obviously chose Odyssey House and thought, how befitting a name. His recent trials and tribulations resembled every bit of an odyssey, and perhaps, through divine intervention, he finally ran out of road and reached a dead end. He was grateful he would have a roof over his head and it wasn't inside a prison. However, his old lifestyle was about to change in ways he never could imagine.

CHAPTER SEVEN

Odyssey House began as the brainchild of Dr. Judianne Densen-Gerber, a groundbreaking clinical psychiatrist who developed the concept of peer-driven group therapy in a residential setting – and without the use of drugs like methadone – to treat and rehabilitate drug addicts. Ray certainly didn't fall into that category. Sure, he'd done his fair share of experimenting with a variety of mind-altering substances over the years, and enjoyed every minute of it, but he did not consider himself an addict by any stretch.

Ray would be placed in the inaugural group of 17 residents living full-time in a locked-down home, sober and celibate, adhering to a set of strict rules and regulations, with restricted access to the outside world, including family and friends. He would have to follow a highly regimented daily schedule involving group therapy and personal counseling, performing household chores and responsibilities, recreational activities, and interpersonal and life skills training.

Ray got all of that information from his detective driver while riding in the back seat of an unmarked police car over the GW Bridge and into

Manhattan. He hadn't seen the city in a while and it looked gorgeous all lit up at night, reflecting its magnificence in the mighty Hudson River. They parked in front of a lovely brownstone that had a tiny flower garden in front protected by black wrought iron fencing. A sign in the lobby reading "Welcome Home!" greeted him as he hesitantly took his first steps over the threshold and into this brand new world. He wasn't feeling particularly welcome at the moment and had no idea what was in store, despite everything he heard on his ride over.

A counselor approached and introduced himself as Perry, and officially took Ray into custody. He would essentially become Ray's shadow until he learned the ropes and adjusted to group home life. Then, it would be a matter of simply co-existing with his fellow residents and the staff each day.

There were some good and bad days in the following weeks and months. Intense screaming and yelling, fist fights, stealing, physical punishments for breaking the rules and seemingly petty offenses. It was similar to a military-style boot camp and the counselors fashioned themselves as drill instructors. If residents behaved and followed orders, they weren't hassled much. Act up and they'd feel the counselor's wrath.

Even though the foundation of Odyssey House was addiction treatment without using drugs, every resident was prescribed some kind of antipsychotic medication that kept them under complete control. Ray dutifully lined up with the other poor souls every day for his thioridazine pill, which was prescribed after he was observed having a few of those intense acid flashbacks. Somehow he knew deep inside it was quickly and drastically turning him into a completely different human being. He walked around in a perpetual zombie-like state, barely functioning, and showing little interest in socializing or even reading a book. Any time he wasn't in therapy, working, or eating, he laid in his bed staring blankly at the ceiling.

What really gnawed at Ray was discovering a freaky new side effect from the thioridazine he was forced to take.

At random times during the day, his body would suddenly start trembling and jerking uncontrollably. The spasming affected his jaws, mouth, lips and tongue, as well as his torso and extremities.

It became serious enough to earn Ray a number of visits to the office of the founder and headmistress herself.

Dr. Densen-Gerber was taking a special interest in Ray's case based on the reports she was hearing from the staff. After several one on one meetings, she diagnosed his disorder as tardive dyskinesia, a serious and sometimes permanent side effect of antipsychotic medications. It causes abnormal, involuntary facial tics and movements, such as sticking the tongue out or making like a fish with the mouth, lips, and jaws.

The doctor told Ray he'd be taken off the medication immediately and she would personally monitor his mental health. There was a connection there with Ray that she didn't often make with her patients. She sensed he was not the typical hard core, strung-out street junkie, or a repeat offender with one last chance. She could read people fairly well and could tell he was a gentle spirit and a good soul. Nonetheless, the program was Ray's punishment and she was responsible for his rehabilitation and for him doing his time. There was no way she would be successful if he were kept so heavily medicated.

During the ensuing months, Ray had a standing weekly appointment with Dr. Judianne for a psych evaluation, which was usually followed by a lively and thoughtful discussion on a topic of mutual interest.

Occasionally, the conversation turned to spirituality and religion, and they were pleasantly surprised to find common ground on the subject of Christian Science. Its founder, Mary Baker Eddy, defined it as "the law of God... the law of Good." It espouses the superiority of the spiritual over the physical; that our reality is purely spiritual and the material world is merely some kind of an illusion.

Dr. Judianne talked about her childhood experiences planting and tending a vegetable and herb garden each spring with her grandfather at his upstate farm. It gave her an appreciation for the sun that gives light, the rains that provide nourishment, and the rich, fertile earth from which new life bursts forth. That was her introduction to a brand new spiritual part of life beyond just attending Mass and going to confession.

"Did you have a garden when you were growing up, Raymond?", she asked.

"I think we tried it one summer, but it was a disaster. Barely any rain, and we always forgot to water, and then the weeds took over. My folks said it wasn't worth the hassle."

He remembered his mother planting some color along their walkway every now and then, and she took care of the few plants they had around the house. but she definitely was not blessed with a green thumb.

"Growing and gardening is still a passion of mine, and I spend as much of my spare time as I can working in my gardens and greenhouse. Would you like to see?" she asked.

"I would love to," he answered, and followed her down a hallway to a padlocked door. She unlocked it and they walked up a few flights of stairs leading to another locked door. When she unlocked and pushed it open, they saw daylight. And suddenly, as big as life- her private garden inside a huge rooftop greenhouse.

Ray had never seen anything like it and was simply awestruck at the concept of an urban garden. It was a brand new concept of utilizing otherwise useless rooftop space as a way for people to grow their own food and know where it came from. Dr. Judianne explained that just about everything that was growing there was being used for the house in some way.

"Our fruits and vegetables, all the herbs and spices we use in cooking the food you eat, these wonderful botanicals and succulents that have medicinal value, all come from here. Then everything gets composted and it's re-used as an organic fertilizer to grow more plants and vegetables. Gramps called it sustainability. It's a continuous cycle that can sustain us, as long as we do it properly."

Dr. Judianne gave Ray a tour of her cherished gardens and greenhouse, and he saw for himself exactly where the lettuce and cucumbers in his salads, and the carrots and onions in his beef stew, came from. He never would have guessed it could be on the rooftop of a brownstone on 109th Street in East Harlem of all places.

When they reached the garden planted with all manner of cacti and succulents, Dr. Judianne directed Ray's attention to a section of slender, spiny-edged plants she considered extra special because of their built-in natural healing properties. She asked Ray if he knew what they were. He had no clue.

"These are called aloe veras, specifically *aloe vera barbadensis*. Now, there are many types of aloes, Raymond, and all of them magnificently attractive in their own special ways. But the *aloe vera barbadensis* variety is the cream of the crop of aloes and that's because there's a special something inside."

Dr. Judianne broke off a leaf and ran her thumbnail down the middle of it, splaying it wide open, revealing a clear, slimy substance oozing onto her fingers. She explained that this gel is used topically to heal a wound or treat sunburn, and can also be taken internally for a number of ailments.

Ray wanted to hear more but Dr. Judianne had appointments and was out of time. As they descended the stairs, Dr. Judianne had an idea. Why not use the garden as therapy for Ray? It would keep him mentally and physically occupied, and he preferred to be alone anyway since he had little in common with his fellow residents. Plus, the garden was getting to be too much to manage for one person and she could use two extra hands and a strong back.

"What would you think about working here with me a few hours a day, Raymond? Does that have any appeal to you?"

He answered, "Are you kidding me? Wow, I'd love it! I think it would be good for me to be working with my hands, and have something productive that I can look forward to. And, I bet you can use a hand up here."

They agreed to keep Ray's exclusive gardening therapy their little secret. Many times during a meal, Ray wanted to proudly proclaim to the group, "I grew that tomato you're eating right here on this roof!" but had to stifle himself lest he blow his cover and jeopardize losing his special gig. The opportunity provided by Dr. D made his time there far more bearable, and working alone kept him from potentially engaging in conflicts with the residents and staff. He relished Dr. Judianne's friendship and mentorship more and more with each passing day, and she was starting to notice a great deal of personal growth and potential in him. In her estimation, the garden therapy idea turned out quite successfully.

As Ray was approaching the conclusion of his two-year sentence, opportunity was knocking on his door once again, and Dr. Judianne hoped and prayed he was now prepared to answer it.

CHAPTER EIGHT

The first few weeks at Odyssey House were on the rocky side for Ray. He wasn't used to rising at dawn and trying to co-exist 24 hours a day with 16 strangers, or adhering to a strict schedule where every hour of his day was spoken for. He was none too thrilled about having to mop the floors, and scrubbing toilets made him gag. He despised the endless group therapy sessions that he considered worthless and a waste of time, and which often turned into screaming contests between counselors and patients. Mostly, though, he felt miserable and down in the dumps over the fact that he hadn't seen or spoken to Silka in weeks.

By watching her prepare elaborate gourmet meals for him, Ray knew his way around a kitchen, and fortunately, no one else did. Those skills earned him much respect from the house and protected him from becoming the victim of any occasional rough stuff. They didn't want the goose that laid the golden egg to get injured because that would be the end of Denver omelets for breakfast.

He tried hard to follow the military-style routine and keep his nose clean, and most of the time there were no issues. He mellowed with each passing day and gradually adapted well to this strange new world into which he was suddenly thrust. Eventually, Ray's winning smile and pleasant personality won over just about everyone, including the formerly stiff and sour-pussed staff. It was hard to explain, but everybody seemed to get along better, and the temperature of the house was lower, when Ray was in the picture, and they all knew it.

So did Dr. Judianne. She discreetly observed his interactions with others, following orders, and the sensible manner in which he dealt with random house drama that cropped up in group therapy sessions. He was patient, respectful, pitched in around the house wherever he could, and always projected a positive attitude that others picked up and began trying themselves. She recognized when that kind of energy catches on and permeates throughout, it makes everyone's life easier. It reminded Dr. J of a simple phrase that Gramps spoke when someone or something makes a tremendous impact for the common good. He used to say, "a rising tide ifts all boats," and she never forgot that powerful image and the wisdom behind those words.

It became obvious that Ray was fast becoming that rising tide. Since the first day they met in her office, Dr. J sensed there was something extra special about him. She couldn't put her finger on it just yet, but she felt there was a spark in him that, when ignited, could set the world on fire. He made steady progress in the program and learned the ropes quickly once the haze of thioridazine was lifted and he was able to think clearly.

At their next session, Dr. Judianne got right down to business and laid her cards on the table.

"Raymond, we won't be working in the greenhouse today." Ray asked if something was wrong.

"No, I want to talk to you about a very serious matter. We'd like you to consider staying on with us and becoming a member of the staff," she told him with a big smile on her face. "We need a junior counselor we can train, and we think you are a perfect example of our program's success. You're living proof that this therapeutic approach to rehabilitation does in fact work."

Ray was gobsmacked. "I don't know, I never thought of myself as a counselor," he sheepishly replied , "and I'm not sure I'm ready to do that job."

Dr. J reassured him he could and would be the ideal choice. He already went through the program, came out the other side, and would serve as an excellent role model for new patients. Up until this meeting, Ray didn't know what he would do or where he would go once he walked out that front door. Everything was up in the air, and anything was on the table. His new life was a blank canvas just waiting for him to paint his very own masterpiece.

"I'd appreciate some time to think it over, if that's OK," Ray asked. "No doubt, it's a humbling offer. But it's also a monumental decision. I imagine it to be a far different experience working as staff."

"Of course, Raymond. Take a few days and then we'll meet again to discuss your decision. But please don't allow fear to make the decision for you. Fear of decision-making, fear of failing, and even fear of success. Fear and worry are everyone's most formidable enemies. There will always be risks in life and fear won't make them go away. It really comes down to whether or not you would enjoy this line of work and find it gratifying and fulfilling. It takes a special type of individual who is naturally equipped with the skills we look for in our counselors, and you happen to possess them."

She advised Ray to pray for guidance and think carefully about the opportunity he's being handed. They don't come along very often in life, and may never again, she cautioned. Ray was shocked, flattered, and trying to wrap his head around what was taking place at that moment. When he finally quieted down and pushed his fear to the side, he saw it for what it actually was: recognition and reward for his exemplary behavior and positive attitude. In other words, he played nice with others.

Then worry wormed its way into Ray's subconscious, questioning whether all of that positive energy would change when he stood on the other side of the fence. It was a valid question, and one that suddenly put his self-confidence to the test. Dr. Judianne always believed in him so he had to find the courage to believe in himself. He didn't want to let her down after all she'd done for him, nor would she be doing it if didn't feel comfortable with it.

Metaphorically speaking, the wise doctor used her rooftop garden and greenhouse therapeutically to plant the seed of personal growth in Raymond. Now was the time for its great emergence and cultivation.

CHAPTER NINE

Perry tapped on Ray's door and asked if he was ready to go. With Dr. J's permission, and Perry acting as his shadow, they arranged a day to travel downtown to Ray's old place so he could try to get some information on Silka's whereabouts. Today was that day.

They rode the F Train downtown, got off and then walked a few blocks to the old apartment. When Ray first saw it, for the first time in years, he felt a twinge in his gut and his heartbeat quickened. The place set the stage for a marvelous and unforgettable chapter of his life, and he had the good fortune of spending it there with a remarkable woman who taught him how to become the best version of himself.

They entered the brownstone and climbed a few flights of stairs to his floor, the sound of their footsteps echoing throughout the cavernous hallway. They stopped in front of #777 and Ray pulled out his key. As soon as he slid it into the lock and couldn't turn it, he was crestfallen and just dropped his chin against his chest, not saying a word. He didn't have to. His reaction spoke volumes.

"I'm sorry about that, Ray," Perry said consolingly. "I could tell she was your soul mate, the way you talked about her in group."

"Man, I tell you what, as heartbroken as I am right now, I still feel she's the love of my life," Ray said dejectedly. "I'll keep trying to find her and see if she'll ever forgive me, and maybe let me have another chance to earn back her love and respect."

It was a somber return trip home, but it gave Ray some quiet time to think. Before he gave Dr. J his final decision, he wanted to know exactly where things stood with Silka. As far as family, except for brother Simon, he was practically disowned and ostracized. They were convinced he was nothing more than a heavyweight drug dealer and a born loser. Ray had no real place to call home, and definitely didn't want to be on the streets with no money or a job. He got to thinking, if they believed in him, and trained him right, joining the staff as a junior counselor just might be what the doctor ordered to get him back up on the good foot and give him a fresh start. Perhaps it was worth taking a stab at it.

Later that afternoon, Dr. Judianne summoned Ray to her office and asked if he had made a decision.

"This place is the closest thing I have to a home, and I feel like I'm part of a family that actually cares about me," he replied, "especially you. If I didn't say yes, I'd be letting both of us down, and that's the last thing I want to do after all you've done for me. I'll be eternally grateful for that."

"You put in the effort that made it possible and the success it is, so bully for you, Raymond," she answered with a beaming smile. "Once you're settled in and more familiar with the group, I'd like you to select a person you believe would benefit from mentoring, much like I did for you. I want to see you pass that on to someone else."

Dr. J assured him he would continue to have access to the rooftop gardens, and she would make the necessary arrangements for his mentor once Ray found a suitable candidate. They sealed the deal with a handshake and a bear hug, and Ray returned to his room, no longer a drug rehab patient but an honest-to-goodness staff counselor. He couldn't have imagined in his wildest dreams the dramatic turn of events in his life over the past couple of years, both good and bad. It was a reassuring reminder that God had a plan in store for him and somehow this past couple of years of craziness was part of it.

It took time for Ray to adjust to his new position and look at life inside the house from an entirely different perspective. He was gradually learning the counselor ropes, and enjoying his interaction with the residents for the most part. There were occasional shoving matches, physical scraps and nose-to-nose "disagreements," but he witnessed those situations before in his group therapy sessions, and watched the way his counselors dealt with them. The lesson was that actions have consequences, and bad behavior results in punishment and house restrictions. Violators learned that quickly and rarely were they repeat offenders.

Modeling his favorite counselors' behavior was a big help in transitioning from resident to staffer. The bottom line was about respect – earning theirs and showing them yours. Seemed simple but that didn't mean it was always easy. The job could be mellow one day, then explosive the next. It was a roller coaster ride for the most part, but he was accustomed to living in a fluid environment where the temperature could reach the boiling point at the drop of a hat.

Ray had the garden for refuge when he needed it, and a few books and science journals that he read to relax and decompress, but something that he always loved was missing from his life. He hadn't picked up a guitar in years and, now that he was on staff, he wanted to get back to playing again. He might even suggest to Dr. Judianne that music might be another form of therapy that could be incorporated in the residents' treatment.

With a steady paycheck, and nowhere to spend it, Ray had saved enough to afford a cheap guitar. On his next day off, he took a trip downtown to Manny's Music, a well-known Manhattan guitar store on W. 48th Street that he often frequented during his playing days with Gulliver. At any given moment, he might find himself standing next to legendary musicians like Bob Dylan, or John Sebastian of the Lovin' Spoonful, Beatle John Lennon, or The Band's Garth Hudson. He walked over and stood in front of a wall with hundreds of new and used acoustic guitars on display from floor to ceiling. He had his eye on a mahogany-top Washburn six-string acoustic when barely within earshot, he heard a strangely familiar voice.

As it got closer, he heard, "Windy? That you?"

Only three other people knew him by that nickname, and it was Adam who most often referred to him with that moniker.

Ray was trying to process the moment and stood in stunned silence, his mouth agape. It was unfathomable to him how the hand of fate could cause their paths to cross again after all these years, on that exact day, and at precisely that time, and in a music store in New York City of all places. A couple of minutes either way and their impromptu reunion never would have occurred.

When Ray finally composed himself, he called out Adam's name and greeted him with a handshake and a hug.

Ray explained he spent the past two years at Odyssey House and was presently on staff there as a junior counselor. He was now living a sober life, but missed playing music so he came down to Manny's to buy a guitar.

Adam told him Gulliver disbanded awhile back and everyone went their separate ways. He was writing songs and recording a demo to shop around to record companies, still in dogged pursuit of rock and roll fame and fortune. He then struck a more serious tone and told Ray that Silka had recently contacted him. She asked if he knew how to get in touch with Ray but unfortunately he didn't know where he was and couldn't help her.

"So then I ask her what she's been up to and there's this really long silence," Adam said. "She then proceeds to tell me she's a patient in the Utica Insane Asylum. A judge sentenced her there after she was found guilty of killing her terminally ill mother."

Ray's knees buckled and he swallowed hard. "No, no, no, it just can't be. No, not her, man. She would never think of doing something like that to her mother. She loved her and always took good care of her."

"Brace yourself, Windy, I'm afraid there's more, and it's pretty gruesome," Adam continued. "I checked into it and found out Silka was charged with murder after the coroner determined her mother was suffocated. Turns out she got a few friends and relatives together and they held what's called a smother party, which apparently is something her people did in the old country for their loved ones who were terminally ill. Their version of euthanasia."

"What?? No way! You gotta' be joking." He was so loud that every head in the place turned toward them.

"No, really, they cover their loved one with a mattress, then everybody gets completely blotto, and they all sit on top of the mattress, and sing songs and tell stories until she's gone, no longer breathing. Incredibly sad and weird, but yeah, unfortunately it's true."

"That's sick, man. How could they do something that bizarre and cruel?" asked Ray.

"Silka told me her mother insisted on it. She didn't want to live anymore and wanted to be put out of her misery so everyone could get on with their lives instead of taking care of her. Silka wanted no part of it, but if a blood relative demanded it, she was obligated to honor the request and uphold the family's traditions.

Following a criminal investigation, Silka was arrested, tried and found guilty of her mother's murder. The judge presiding over her case found her actions to be psychotic and deranged, and considered her a danger to herself and others. Since there wasn't anyone to care for her, he sentenced her to an upstate New York facility for the criminally insane.

CHAPTER TEN

After Adam dropped that bombshell on him, Ray had difficulty re-focusing his attention on his original mission – buying a guitar. Adam said he was sorry he had to be the bearer of such awful news, but felt Ray should know the truth about Silka and her whereabouts. He apologized for having to cut their visit short, because he had an appointment and was in a hurry, so they quickly exchanged phone numbers and said an awkward goodbye, promising to stay in touch.

The euphoria that comes with scoring a brand new guitar was dulled by the freight train of ugly thoughts running amok in Ray's now shattered brain. Through scuttlebutt at the house, he hadn't heard glowing reviews about the place where Silka would likely live out the rest of her years. There were reports of inmates being beaten, shackled, shocked, raped, drugged, and thrown in solitary confinement. Misdiagnosed as criminally insane, yet in reality simply a dutiful daughter reluctantly carrying out her mother's final wishes, Silka was now an innocent lamb trying to stay alive among a pack of ravenous wolves – the worst of the worst psychopaths and sociopaths who've been found guilty of unspeakable atrocities.

It was all Ray could think about, but he found the fortitude to momentarily push those sordid thoughts aside so he could make his selection. He chose a white-on-black Epiphone that sounded sweet and was within his budget, and they threw in a set of strings and a cheap guitar case to transport it home. Ray was anxious to get playing again, but Silka's saga was a dark, stormy cloud over his head and a major distraction. As bad as he felt, he couldn't imagine the horrors she was suffering.

Within a few days, Ray had new strings on the guitar and it was tuned up and ready to play. It would take time for him to regain the rock hard calluses on his fingers, and relearn his chords and scales. He practiced whenever he had a chance to squeeze in 15 minutes here or a half-hour there. Soon he became confident and proficient enough to perform a few old tunes for the house from his Gulliver days. They loved singing along, clapping their hands and stomping their feet to add a bit of percussion. A few of them asked Ray if he'd be willing to give them lessons, and he was happy to oblige them. The staff noticed that much like gardening therapy, music, with its soothing and relaxing effects, and ability to break down barriers, could be yet another tool in the therapy tool box. It soon became part of Odyssey House's recovery and rehab program and they had Ray to thank for it.

There wasn't a doubt in anyone's mind whether or not Ray was working out as a new staff member. For some reason, the residents seemed to respond more positively to him than some of the veteran counselors on staff who were impressed by his sensitivity, compassion and natural ability to communicate. He gladly went the extra mile by playing his guitar and cooking gourmet meals for them, and simply tried his damndest to give them the same level of care he received during his time there as a resident inmate. They recognized his dedication and commitment to helping them get better, and it inspired and motivated them.

Ray was in his room practicing his scales one afternoon when there was a rap on the door. Perry popped his head in and told Ray he had a telephone call.

"Did they say who's calling?" asked Ray.

"I think he said his name was Aaron or Allen, something like that," Perry answered.

Ray figured out it could be Adam. He rushed down the hallway to the pay phone and picked up the receiver that was dangling by its cord.

Ray shouted, "Hello, Adam? Is this Adam?"

That old familiar voice sounded a might subdued. "Hey, Windy, how's life treating you?"

"I can't really complain, you know. I'm working and finally have some stability in my life now. I miss the music though, but not that crazy life."

"I hear ya', Windy. And glad you're doing OK. But hey, listen, I don't want to bring you down but I'm afraid I have to give you some bad news again...."

"Oh no, please don't tell me it's Silka," Ray pleaded, his voice quivering in fear of what Adam was about to reveal.

"Unfortunately, yes, it's about Silka. She's gone, man, I'm sorry to have to tell you," Adam sadly replied.

Ray asked, "Gone where? Where'd they take her?"

"Windy, she didn't go anywhere. They found her dead in her bed."

Ray looked grimly at the floor in silence and shook his head from side to side. It was part shock and disbelief, part sadness and grief, and a dash of regret and remorse all rolled up in one. Finally, he asked Adam if he knew what happened or had any details.

"I read that she was killed by some psycho inmate who was already in there serving time for murder," Adam offered.

"Murdered? How in God's name did that happen?"

Adam paused for a few seconds to collect himself before delivering the tragically ironic news.

"The guy snuck into her room and put a pillow over her face while she was sleeping and suffocated her. Can you believe it?"

"Poor Silka, she didn't deserve any of this," Ray replied angrily. "What a cruel ending to a life that had so much promise. We were so in love, but I know I disappointed her, and I'll always regret that I didn't have the chance to make it up to her."

"Whether things turn out good or bad, or happy or sad, it's all part of God's master plan, Windy. You were the one who taught me that."

Ray nodded and suggested they meet up soon for coffee and some face time to help cheer him up. He hung up the phone and returned to his room to ponder the heavy conversation he just had. He felt like he was just awakening from a scary dream and trying to recall the fuzzy details. Adam's call was mind blowing to say the least, but Ray also appreciated the courage it took to give him that dreadful news. It had to have been tough for Adam to do, and it demonstrated to Ray the importance Adam placed on their friendship, and the responsibilities and obligations that come with it. Realizing that took some sting out of the pain Ray was feeling in his heart.

Ray said a prayer for the repose of Silka's life-pouring soul and for God's mercy on her passage into His kingdom. He vowed to do everything in his power to get there himself so he may once again feast his eyes on her exquisite beauty and hear the love in her sweet voice.

The next few weeks put Ray's character to the ultimate test and challenged his ability to handle adversity like the horrible death of his soul mate. Not surprisingly, he was experiencing mood swings and showing signs of mild depression, yet still managing to keep his wits about him and meet his work responsibilities. He had a few extra sessions with Dr. Judianne to work through the grieving process, and kept his mind occupied by playing guitar and trying his hand at songwriting. He had a lot of material to work with and a ton of pent up emotion to get out his system.

Still, he would occasionally drift off into a daydream, and in his mind's eye, rerun snippets of the precious moments in time they were lucky enough to experience together. They both felt theirs was truly a match made in heaven that took a perilous U-turn and crashed and burned in hell. It was going to take Ray awhile to sort it all out and try and make sense of it, if that were even possible.

One morning while eating breakfast, Dr. Judianne stopped in the kitchen and asked Ray if he would come to her office when he was done with his meal. Something had come up that she wanted to discuss with him. He thought it might involve the gardens, or have something to do with the music therapy program he was helping to develop. He made his way to her office and stood outside her open door.

"Yes, Raymond, please come in and sit down. I have a serious matter to discuss with you," she said in her soft and gentle voice.

"Did I do something wrong, or didn't do something I should have?" Ray asked.

She responded with an emphatic "no," it was nothing he did. It was somebody else. Ray asked who she meant.

"Raymond, it's your brother, Simon. Your father called earlier and told me Simon took his own life today. He said you two were very close, and he didn't know how to tell you, so he asked if I would. I'm so sorry for your loss, and you and your family have my deepest sympathies."

The color drained from Ray's face and he turned white as a sheet. Then suddenly, his eyes teared up and he burst out wailing, pounding his fists on the armrests and stomping his feet. He became so distraught that snot was running down his nose and he was drooling like a dog begging for a bone. The doctor settled him down and explained that it was important for him to be strong for his family and to make sure Simon is shown the dignity and respect he deserves.

Ray was excused from his duties to take a week of bereavement, surrounded by his family, relatives, friends and neighbors. Over the course of his many conversations with them at Simon's wake and funeral, he learned that his brother had grown increasingly despondent and withdrawn the past few months, and finally decided he'd reached his limit of physical and mental torment. His parents discovered him in his wheelchair, in the garage with the door closed and his father's car engine running. Carbon monoxide poisoning. Death comes quickly.

Ray could barely imagine what he was hearing but at the same time had an inkling that Simon was struggling. He was now smothering himself in a blanket of guilt about not being there more often to provide the moral support Simon needed. Simon would have told him not to waste his time feeling sorry for himself and keep moving on, doing whatever God intended for you.

Even though they only saw one another infrequently, Ray was going to miss Simon's brotherly love and his God-given gift of wisdom that he was happy to share with anyone who bothered asking. Even when Simon was a young child, people would comment that he was wise beyond his years. But was never a wise guy.

It was time for Ray to accept Simon's directive and return to his life at Odyssey House. He needed the structure and support after suffering through the heart-wrenching deaths of the two people in life who were closest to him. A converted optimist, he had to find a way to turn the bitter taste of lemons into the refreshing sweetness of lemonade. He knew he had to start looking on the bright side or he too might follow the same path and suffer the same fate as Simon. He wasn't sure how or what to do, so he prayed he would find the same inner strength and courage that his brother always modeled, at least up until he reached his breaking point.

CHAPTER ELEVEN

A litany of sympathies, condolences, apologies, and prayers of consolation were showered upon Ray when he walked back into Odyssey House, and it gave him a warm and welcomed feeling like it was his home. Being around his mother and father was always so toxic, and witnessing their constant mania and bickering wasn't good for his own temperament and mental health. Indeed, as their remaining son, he felt obligated to be there for them in their time of grief, but by the same token, he realized he wouldn't be much help when he himself was a basket case overflowing with anxiety and stress.

Ray didn't find that dark cloud of dysfunction and toxicity at Odyssey House. Certainly, there were intense disagreements, bad behavior, and a few regrettable moments, just like any family or household might experience. As is the case in most families, the tempest in the teapot blows over, and the parties involved eventually make nice and place the unfortunate incident in the history books. That was the difference between Odyssey House and the Fineman house, where the weather was perpetually stormy and the inhabitants never learned how to play well with others.

Over the next few months, Ray experienced the five stages of grief: denial, anger, bargaining, depression and acceptance - whether he was aware of it or not. Dr. Judianne was personally guiding him through the delicate process and saw that he was still fragile, yet making progress. There was no denying he'd endured a boatload of trauma that most people could never imagine, much less survive. But working together, they concentrated on righting his listing ship; plugging the holes in the hull, and tuning up a sputtering engine that would allow the captain of the ship to be underway again. They could feel the winds of change were beginning to pick up once more, and as every sailor worth his salt knows, one must take advantage of favorable conditions when they present themselves.

On a rainy and dreary fall afternoon, when everyone was stuck inside the lounge and doing nothing but killing time and burning daylight, Ray read the room and felt the mood could use some brightening. He grabbed his guitar and just started randomly singing and playing a few riffs. He called it noodling. If only momentarily, the live music Ray was creating on the spot, right in front of their very eyes, had this enormous power to take people's minds off their assorted worries, faults, hang-ups, quirks, failures, and idiosyncrasies. They entered this ethereal dimension where all of the baggage sloughs off and vanishes, and for a moment, they are transported somewhere else. They suddenly aren't thinking about who they are, what they've done wrong, and how they ever allowed themselves to get to this place.

As Ray was playing, he caught Perry out of the corner of his eye standing off in the corner, discreetly trying to give him the high sign to wrap up or take a break. He obviously had something important to tell

Ray. When he finished the tune, he excused himself from the group and walked over to Perry to ask what was going on.

"I was just told we're having an all-hands staff meeting in 30 minutes," he explained. "I have no idea what it could be about, but I guess we'll find out soon."

A half-hour later, the entire staff filed solemnly into a large conference room and took seats around a table that looked the size of a football field. A din fell over the room with everyone fretting and surmising over the purpose of the emergency meeting. The murmuring ceased the moment Dr. Densen-Gerber entered.

"OK folks, I'm not going to tiptoe through the tulips here or beat around the bush," she announced. "It's a sad day here and one I never thought would arrive. Odyssey House was purchased by one of our competitors and they will be bringing in their own people. They made it clear they won't have a need to retain any of our present staff."

A few gasps and muffled sobs were heard, but otherwise, radio silence. Nobody could find the words that would possibly express the full measure of their shock and disbelief at hearing her announcement.

"I am just as numb as you are," she continued in a shaky voice. "I just found out about it last night when I received a call from one of the board of directors informing me they had voted to accept a purchase offer from some big time investor group. Although I'm not on the board, as one of the founders of Odyssey House, I felt I deserved more respect than that.

"It is with my sincerest regret that I must inform you that your positions will be terminated as of 5 pm tomorrow, and you will receive severance pay based on your years of service. I'll assist you with your job searches to the extent I'm able, and want you all to know how much I've appreciated your loyalty, your dedication to your work, and our years together proving this rehabilitative therapy model works. Now, I have to leave before I start bawling."

Ray looked at Perry as if to say, "this is a dream, right? Am I in the twilight zone, living in another dimension, or is what I think is happening really happening?"

Without speaking, everyone rose from their seats almost in unison and filed out of the room in stunned silence, some looking down, some shaking their heads in amazement and disbelief, a few of the old timers whining over their lives and careers being turned topsy-turvy in the blink of an eye without the slightest inkling it was happening.

God, what's next? Ray wondered. It was one calamity after another, starting with the mind-bending, brain cell-destroying LSD trip, and getting booted from the band. Then, his separation from Silka, and Simon's pool accident and paralysis. That was followed by a drug bust for dealing pot and being sentenced to a rehab for a couple of years. Silka gets institutionalized for murdering her mother, then she's suffocated in her bed by a psychotic inmate. On top of all that, his dear brother Simon takes his life. Now, his job and a group of people he truly had grown to cherish, possibly even more than playing guitar in a rock and roll band, would no longer serve as the anchor that kept his life from going adrift. A tidal wave of madness and misfortune had crashed down on him, and he could barely keep his head above water, gasping for air to stay alive.

A hit song by the band Cream that Ray always appreciated because of its humorous and clever play on words helped him put things in perspective for the moment and poke fun at his disastrous plight at the same time. The song was "Born Under a Bad Sign," and the lyric that he felt perfectly summed up his life at that particular point in time went thusly:

ALOE MAN

Born under a bad sign
I've been down since I began to crawl
If it wasn't for bad luck
I wouldn't have no luck at all.

Ray couldn't get that song out of his head. As horrible as life seemed, he had a strange feeling that his luck was about to change.

CHAPTER TWELVE

"Be bold, Raymond, and always dream big," exhorted Dr. Judianne as they met for the final time before their departure from Odyssey House.

"You know, real adventure begins when you find yourself out of your comfort zone and flying by the seat of your pants," she continued. "I did that when I started this program. Surely, it's a little nerve-wracking, but also quite exhilarating and every bit the adventure."

Ray admitted he had no idea what his immediate plans were, but he was praying extra hard that God would give him answers to the endless stream of questions running through his head.

"Well, Raymond, you're still a young man, and you have time to do something meaningful with your life with what you've learned here. Try to imagine your future as a blank canvas, and my wish is for you to go out there and paint your masterpiece."

Ray smiled and thanked her for setting a new course for his life at Odyssey House. He promised he would do something that would make her proud someday. She smiled back and told him he just did.

"I'll never forget everything you've taught me, but more than anything, you showed me that you actually cared about my well-being.

You could have looked at me as just another patient doing time, going through the motions, completing a sentence, but you didn't. You saw something deep inside me that I didn't know was there, and you brought it to the surface. It was my confidence. Your encouragement and support gave me confidence. And I'm sure gonna' need it."

Ray planned to take a bus to Jersey that evening and stay with his folks until he figured out his next move. Everything was on the table, including leaving it all behind if he felt there was an opportunity elsewhere. Sol and Myrna were still showing signs of both aggression and depression over their son's death, so Ray was keenly aware of the need to tread lightly. They had short fuses and he didn't want to be the one striking the match.

As soon as he arrived, they went into the kitchen and Myrna brewed a pot of coffee and sliced a piece of blueberry pie for everyone.

"I spoke to your sister yesterday and she wants you to call her," Sol blurted. "We told her what's been happening and she immediately started crying, and said she needs to talk to you as soon as you got here. She sounded very upset."

Ray promised he would call her after dinner, and then asked if they'd heard from anyone else.

"We got a call out of the blue from your cousin Dupree, who's driving an 18-wheeler over the road now," Sol said. "He's passing through the area and wanted to stop by and visit for a spell. Been a long time since we've seen him."

Ray estimated it was 20 years or more, when Dupree was just a little squirt. Ray was quite a bit older but didn't pay much attention to their age difference, and he recalled they got along pretty well together. He wondered what a grown-up version looked and behaved like, and all these years later, what he's done with his life. He'd find out tomorrow at dinner.

Ray anxiously dialed his sister Bonnie Lee, with whom he hadn't spoken in a coon's age. Theirs was an on-again, off-again sibling rivalry, but at the end of the day, they were related by blood and wouldn't think twice about shedding it for the other if the situation demanded it. She was estranged from the family for quite some time after eloping with a jarhead. For years, no one in the family knew where she was or how to contact her, and then, out of the blue, she happened to call right at the time when her brother was due to visit.

The moment she said hello in her gentle and comforting tone, Bonnie Lee's voice still hit Ray hard, like a Mack truck. She sounded exactly the way he remembered. He greeted her with excitement and told her how happy he was to be finally reconnecting after so long.

"That's what I wanted to talk to you about, Ray-Ray," Bonnie Lee said, lovingly using the nickname she teased him with when they were young. "What would you say about moving out to California?"

"California? What would I do? I don't know anybody, have no place to live...."

Bonnie Lee stopped him cold.

"Wrong, Ray-Ray. We just got transferred to Camp Pendleton in California and we have our own place in Oceanside. After me and Dad spoke, we talked it over and well, we'd like you to come out and stay with us until you can find work and get back on your feet."

Dr. Judianne's parting advice to Ray about being bold and dreaming big came rushing back to him. In milliseconds, he had to process his sister's gracious offer, consider all the possibilities, and weigh the risks against the rewards. Dr. J taught him the value of that simple exercise when it came to making any decision. Ray's gut reaction was understandably one of doubt and fear of the unknown, resulting in a moment of queasiness. But then he quickly reminded himself of this newfound wellspring of confidence and self-esteem that he could draw from to destroy any negative thoughts and feelings and replace them with positive ones.

"That's incredibly generous of you guys," Ray gushed. "It really means a lot that you want to help. I don't know what to say, Bonnie Lee. There's so much to think about. That's a major move and an awful big decision. I mean, it sounds cool, but..."

"No ifs, ands or buts, Ray," she snapped back. "No excuses. You're getting a chance to start fresh and make a new life for yourself. And you know if you don't do this now, you never will."

"You're right, as usual," he admitted. "What have I got to lose, really?"

"But also, think of what you have to gain? You'll never know if you don't try. There's only one way to find out!"

They agreed to talk in the next day or so and take Ray's temperature again on the prospect of picking up and moving across the country, and living with his sister and leatherneck brother-in-law. Would he warm up or cool down to the idea after he had time to ponder the pluses and minuses, and carefully weigh the risks and rewards? And was he capable of mustering enough courage and having the *cajones* to leave his familiar old world behind? Could he find the self-confidence to begin building an entirely new existence in a totally unfamiliar world? He needed to sleep on it, thinking maybe the answers would come in his dreams.

The next day, Ray ran a few errands and helped his mother prepare for Dupree's visit later that afternoon. He proudly showed off his newly acquired cooking skills and basically took over the kitchen, peeling potatoes and carrots, and getting a rump roast in the oven. Myrna was overjoyed watching Ray's prowess in the kitchen and the unprecedented culinary spectacle unfolding before her eyes, and savored the fact that she had the night off from cooking.

The doorbell rang, signaling Dupree's arrival because no one ever rang the doorbell. Sol opened the front door and welcomed his nephew with a warm embrace and a few light slaps on the back. Ray and Myrna followed with handshakes, hugs and kisses, and then took his cowboy hat and showed him inside.

"Y'all look fine as frog's hair," Dupree observed with his distinctive Texas twang. "I wasn't sure what to expect after so many years. But first, I wanna say on behalf of mama and daddy how sorry we all were to hear about Simon. Can't imagine what y'all been going through. Must've felt like you got cow-kicked."

They thanked him for the sympathies and then decided they'd celebrate Simon's life with a bottle of Pinot Noir, Simon's preferred vintage. Dupree gave them a brief update on his mama, Myrna's sister Pearlie, who had been seriously ill for a while but was now starting to recover, and then the conversation soon turned to Ray and his pathetic tales of woe. That segued into sister Bonnie Lee's call and her subsequent invitation to pick up and move to the west coast. He told Dupree he was trying to decide whether or not he should go for it.

"You kiddin' me, boy? Shoot, that's a no-brainer. You'd be looney tunes not to. Let me tell you, it's like nirvana out there. Perfect weather. Fun and sun. Gorgeous women. Everywhere you look there's either the ocean, mountains or desert. What's not to like about that?"

"Well, for one thing, I don't have much money left or any transportation to get there…"

"Hey cuz, I could get you at least as far as Nacogdoches! I'm fixin' to head back home in a few days after I drop this load. You could ride with me out to East Texas, and boy howdy, I wouldn't mind having some company. I might even be able to arrange a run to California and give you a lift out there. Whaddya say? Mama would love to see you!"

The room grew painfully quiet for a full minute or more. Ray pursed his lips and didn't utter a peep, feeling the burn from the six eyeballs fixed on him across the room. Then he grinned at Dupree and stated, "OK, you got yourself some company. When do we leave?"

CHAPTER THIRTEEN

Three days later, at the crack of dawn, Ray showed up at Dupree's hotel with his guitar case in hand and a knapsack on his back. They filled up on a big breakfast and made sure to take care of their bathroom business before hitting the road, since there would be no potty breaks or pit stops. Feeling stuffed on top of a nervous stomach, Ray climbed clumsily into the cab of Dupree's 18-wheeler and found a place behind the seat to stow his gear. He tried to calm down and prepare himself mentally for the next few days and nights on the road, riding thousands of miles with someone he hadn't seen in years, despite the fact that it's his first cousin and they were pals as kids. That was eons ago. Who knows, Dupree might be a mean, dirty, obnoxious nut job now. Nonetheless, Ray was all in. In order to remain optimistic, he just kept singing to himself, "California here I come."

Ray didn't have a clue about what was in store during this trip, yet he knew on some level it would likely be an unforgettable, once-in-a-lifetime experience, and just might turn out to be tons of fun. Like it or not, that grown-up version of Dupree that Ray was trying to imagine just a couple of days ago was starting to reveal itself.

Off they went, Dupree at the oversized wheel, double-clutching and working his way through about 10 gears, as Ray bounced in his seat and watched with astonishment how physical the driving was, and how easy he made it look. They were hoping to put in about 1,100 miles for the day and finish up the remaining 500 tomorrow. However, Dupree made it clear there were all kinds of unknown and unforeseen forces at work that could easily throw a wrench in his plan at any time. He tries to stay optimistic and positive, but at the same time, never lets his hopes and expectations get too high.

"Truckers operate under Murphy's Law," he joked. "You know what that means, cuz?"

"Oh yeah! When I was in a touring band and driving all over hell's half-acre, that was the code of the road," Ray shot back in a slightly raised voice to be heard over the din in the cab. "Anything that can go wrong will go wrong, and at the worst possible time. Boy, ain't that the truth."

"Took me a while to get that, ya know? I wasn't paying close enough attention to the real wisdom in those words," Dupree admitted. "But it seems like 'ol Mr. Murphy hit the nail on the head."

Ray thought about it for a minute and then had a revelation.

"You know, I just realized, we were taught the same thing in the Boy Scouts, only it was two words: 'Be Prepared.'

All 18 wheels, 50 feet and 16 tons of this motorized monstrosity were soon barrelling down the New Jersey Turnpike at 60 miles an hour, and soon after that, they were rolling through Delaware and into Maryland's Eastern Shore and across the Chesapeake Bay Bridge. Dupree said they would soon be past the madness of Baltimore and D.C. and back to more civilized driving when they reached Virginia.

Ray was curious about the chatter crackling from Dupree's CB radio, especially some of the strange language they used and couldn't decipher. What the heck are they talking about? "There's a Smoky up ahead taking pictures?"

Dupree explained that means a fellow truck driver ahead of them wants his brethren behind to be on the lookout for a state trooper who is pointing a radar gun at passing vehicles to catch them speeding. He said the law monitors the CBer's channels so the truckers use code words and phrases to throw them off.

Dupree picked up the mic and responded to the tip.

"That's a big 10-4 good buddy. Much obliged. This here's the Gobbler, yeah we're Memphis bound and keeping it on the double nickel for now. Be safe brother."

"That's what your name is on that thing, the Gobbler?" Ray chuckled.

"Yeah, that's my handle alright, good buddy," Dupree replied. "See, my nickname back home is Turkey 'cause I worked at a poultry processing plant killin' and cuttin' up birds. A gobbler is the nickname for a turkey, so I just went with it."

It was close to midnight when Dupree's Freightliner pulled into a Stuckey's Truck Stop right outside of Memphis. They needed food, fuel and a hot shower immediately and in that order. Afterward, they returned to the cab to catch a few hours of sleep before making the final leg home. Dupree took the sleeper, and Ray said he'd just crash right in his seat. But first, he asked Dupree if it was OK to play one quick song on his guitar.

"Sure, cuz," he shot back, then pulled a harmonica from his pants pocket and grinned Texas style – big and wide – as he put it up to his mouth. "Whatcha' wanna' play? I'll just follow you."

"How about that ol' Sam Cooke classic "Bring it on Home to Me"? You know that one?"

"Shoot, that was the first song I learned on this harp," Dupree said. "I played it and Mama sang it."

The impromptu cab jam started off slowly and softly, and they tried hard to keep the volume low, but they locked in and the playing got spirited right away. Before long, Ray was wailing like a sanctified Gospel singer and slamming bar chords on his guitar, and Dupree played the part of a human bellows, inhaling and exhaling into the harp's tiny square reeds with lightning speed, running his mouth up and down that thing like he was devouring an ear of corn.

They played one more tune and called it good for the night so they could sneak in a few hours of kip. There was another 500 miles and about six hours travel time in front of them, unless Murphy decided to rear his ugly head and gum that up. First, they needed to put a few gallons of fuel in their own gas tanks by getting some shuteye.

Ray didn't sleep more than 15 minutes at a time, and was wide awake to watch the sun come up through a dirty, bug-splattered windshield. He sat there piecing together the reality that he'd just driven 1100 miles and slept sitting upright in the cab of a big rig tractor-trailer that's parked at a truck stop in Memphis, Tennessee, a mere stone's throw from the mighty Mississippi River. What a difference a day makes, he thought.

When Dupree awakened from his nap, the two new traveling companions grabbed coffees and a few donuts and hit the road so they'd be ahead of the Memphis morning commute. Within minutes, they reached the foot of the Hernando de Soto Bridge that spans Old Man River, the Big Muddy, whatever people want to call it. They both were bedazzled by the undulating steel arches and the picturesque early morning view from above the river. Ray was floored but couldn't find any words to show it. Dupree said crossing over the Mississippi always gives him a thrill and sends a chill down his spine because of its immense size and scale compared to any other river he's seen. He marvels at its might.

It was smooth sailing all the way to Texarkana and across the Texas state line. The constant chatter from the squawk box provided hours of entertainment for Ray. He was glued to this new contraption, craning his neck toward the speaker so he could hear better and try to figure out what the drivers were saying. In fairly short order, he was translating for Dupree. He explained they were riding in a "Freight Skater" and "putting the hammer down" to make time. There was a "plain brown wrapper" at their "back door" so be sure we don't get caught with our "ears on." Suddenly, he heard something about "reefer." He looked at Dupree and asked if that meant someone was trucking weed. Dupree laughed and spit out the gulp of coffee he'd just taken, which sprayed the windshield and came dripping out of his nose.

Wiping up the mess, he said, "No, cuz'! The reefer they're talking about 'aint the kind you smoke. It's a big rig that's refrigerated. Loaded with perishables. But not those kinds of perishables."

The reefer exchange opened up a new conversation between them about marijuana, including admissions that they both have indulged, although it had been many years since Ray had the opportunity. He talked about his time at Odyssey House, how he got there in the first place, and then how a miscarriage of justice completely changed his life. All without drugs.

"I have a little stash at home, so if you're up for it, we can blaze a few," Dupree said with a big Texas smile he couldn't wipe off his face. "Been a long stretch, and I'm really looking forward to a little down time."

They reached their destination and arrived in Nacogdoches mid-afternoon. Dupree called his mama right away and told her he had a surprise for her and was coming over. He hid Ray in the bushes outside the front door and knocked. As soon as Pearlie opened the door, Ray popped out and yelled, "Surprise, Aunt Pearlie!"

Pearlie looked like she was about to have a heart attack. The color drained from her face, and she was gasping for air and pressing one hand against her chest, too shocked to speak. When she finally was able to gather her thoughts, she screamed Ray's name and wrapped her arms around him. He kissed her on each cheek and gave her a hug, but couldn't get both arms all the way around her. Pearlie sure got big since Ray last laid eyes on her.

She insisted Ray stay with her for a few days and let Dupree catch up on his sleep. They caught one another up on their families and their lives, and their ups and downs, but looked back fondly on the years they spent together before she and her husband Virgil moved away.

Pearlie was an outstanding cook and she fed her boys well the next couple of days. Ray remembered her meatballs and gravy, and how much better they were than his mother's even though they both used the exact same recipe. That night for dinner, guess what was on the table? She knocked it out of the ball park just like before. Taste can be a strong trigger, and biting into one of those baseball-sized bombers brought back a flood of childhood memories Ray forgot about, or never realized had been tucked away for safekeeping all this time.

Feeling refreshed after 20 straight hours of uninterrupted sleep, Dupree came over and joined them for dinner. Afterward, while helping to clear the table, he asked Ray if he's comfortable, and enjoying the home cooking, and Mama's company.

"Hell yes!" he answered. "It's been an awesome couple of days for certain, and all thanks to you. You made it happen."

"No, boys, God made it happen," Pearlie added. "It was His divine hand of fate that brought us all together."

"Well, I sure am sorry to break up this reunion," Dupree said.

What do you mean, Ray asked.

"Like I told you I would, I asked to get on a list for a trip to California once I had my rest time. Thought it might take a week or so, but 'dad gum if they didn't call today. Cuz, we leave for California in two days!"

Pearlie said "Awwww, shoot, I've been enjoying your company so much, dear. Every time I look at you I see the spittin' image of my sister. But always remember everything happens for a reason, and it's all part of His divine plan."

Ray was slightly taken aback by Dupree's announcement and the stark realization that it was all becoming real now. The pieces were falling into place. There was no stopping or turning back now. This was literally where the rubber meets the road.

In 48 hours, Ray would buckle up for the final leg of his cross-country journey and try to pass the time and the miles by envisioning the road ahead and what lies around the next curve. Once again, he was heading blindly but boldly into the unknown, flying solo by the seat of his pants, unsure where the trail begins and where it ends, but confident he was pointed in the right direction: West.

CHAPTER FOURTEEN

The morning of his scheduled departure, Ray woke up and smelled the coffee. The clock read 5:30 and he could hear his aunt moving around in the kitchen preparing their final meal together. He was happy-sad about cutting their visit short, but at the same time grateful for the quality time he was able to spend with her.

There was a cup of coffee and a steaming stack of pancakes already on the table waiting for him when Ray swung open the kitchen door and greeted his Aunt Pearlie with a kiss on the cheek and a hearty good morning. She told him how wonderful it was to see one another again.

"C'mon now, sit down and eat your breakfast while it's still hot," Pearlie instructed. "I remember how much you always loved my pancakes, just like Dupree, so I wanted to make 'em for you as a little going-away present."

"They're incredible Aunt Pearlie, just like I remember," Ray mumbled with his mouth full. "They're amazingly fluffy, like eating big puffs of clouds. Nobody makes them like this. Just as light as a feather."

Ray scarfed down that stack and one more before excusing himself to gather up his belongings. He told Pearlie it was go-time, and thanked her sincerely for her company and gracious hospitality. He admitted to feeling a bit rattled and slightly nervous about his future, but also eager to discover the new horizons that awaited him in California.

For Ray, their impromptu visit was energizing; a screwball of a gift from the Almighty that none of them ever expected or would have imagined. Out of left field, all three just so happened to be inserted serendipitously into each other's lives, and at the same time. Call it plain good luck, sheer coincidence, or intercession from a supreme being, Ray considered it the perfect salve to heal his broken heart and soul, and it came at just the right time. For once, Murphy had it backwards. The best possible thing that could go right, did indeed, and at the best possible time.

They promised each other they'd visit and try to be better at staying in touch. With a few tears welling up in their eyes, they said "so long" rather than "goodbye" with the hope and expectation there would be more visits in the future.

Ray stepped out into pouring rain and was walking away when he heard Pearlie call his name.

"Here Ray, take this here umbrella," she shouted. "You need it to make sure your guitar don't get wet. Just leave it with Dupree to return."

It was just like Aunt Pearlie to always think of others first.

Ray had to hoof it in the rain a few blocks to the local Piggly Wiggly and wait in the parking lot for Dupree and the mighty Freightliner to show up. He was right on time and gave a blast on the horn to let Ray know he'd arrived. Ray climbed up and pulled the door open.

"'Morning, cuz. Welcome aboard. Did Mama make you something good to eat this morning?" Dupree inquired.

Ray gave him the rundown on the breakfast Aunt Pearlie made especially for him. Dupree agreed he must be pretty special because she doesn't make those cloud pancakes for just anybody. He confessed he has to beg her.

Dupree worked the big beast through the local street traffic and soon had them on the freeway headed straight north to connect with I-40, a main corridor running through the hot and barren desert in the hinterlands of West Texas and the Panhandle, New Mexico, Arizona and California. They had many hours and miles in front of them just to reach that point, and then it was another half-day to the New Mexico state line. Breaking out a road atlas, Ray was just now grasping the enormity of the Lone Star state and confirming the claim, made mostly by the people who live there, that everything is bigger in Texas.

"I can start at the bottom of the state and drive for an entire day, 24 hours, and I'd still be in Texas," Dupree stated with a hint of pride since no other state could make that claim.

Instead of listening to the incessant yammering coming from the CB radio, Ray decided he would document the scenes he witnessed with each passing mile and record them in his journal for posterity, or at least to look back on some day and relive the moment in time. His eyes were as big as saucers and his head was on a swivel, soaking it in like a thirsty sponge. He didn't want to overlook a single detail about this venture.

Ray wrote that the view was nothing but 360 degrees of pure sagebrush and prairie, flat as a tabletop and dotted with scrubby patches of mesquite and manzanita trees. Undoubtedly, it was big sky country with vast, wide open spaces all the way to the horizon line. Texas Longhorns and beef cattle were everywhere, fenced in by miles of barbed wire. When the wind blew strong and from the right direction, tumbleweeds tumbled across the highway. And then there were those tall, slender, black A-frame structures that popped up every so often in the middle of nowhere. Ray's inquiring mind wanted to know what they were. He never saw anything that even slightly resembled that.

"Those are bat towers, cuz," Dupree responded. Ray was puzzled by his reply and wondered aloud why someone would build a tower for bats.

"After hunting all night, they return to their roosts, which are usually found under bridges, overpasses, anywhere it's dark and there's protection from the hot sun," Dupree patiently explained. "As you can see, there ain't any bridges or overpasses out here, and bats are a farmer's best friend. They like to keep them around for insect control on their crops, so they build these towers to give them a place to roost during the day. They all come flying out the bottom when it gets dark, ready to start hunting for bugs again. Pretty cool to see."

A lot of the small cities and towns along the way were easily identified by humongous water towers bearing their names, and at times, a clever descriptive motto. Dupree recalled a few that stuck out in his mind from covering nearly every square mile of the state.

"Up in the panhandle, they got Happy, Texas. It's 'The town without a frown.'" Ray cracked up laughing.

"In West Texas, out near Midland-Odessa, there's this tiny little town called Stanton. Theirs is '3,000 friendly people and a few 'ol soreheads.'"

Ray wondered how they got their names. They were funny, strange, outlandish, and almost unbelievable – Cut and Shoot, Muleshoe, Nimrod, Noodle, Bacon, Earth, Poteet, Hooks, and Ding Dong. Ray joked the person who came up with that last name had to be one.

About an hour later, they connected with I-40 and started heading west, pushing through the punishing heat and some of the harshest terrain Ray had ever experienced. Dupree wanted to keep going for a couple of hours and then catch some winks at a truck stop or rest stop. They were making decent time and Dupree still had fuel in the tank, literally and figuratively.

At a truck stop outside of Amarillo, they took a quick nap, filled the gas tank, and grabbed a bite to eat. The sun was just peeking out over the horizon, giving them an early start to the day and a few hours head start before the heat really kicked in. Ray recognized the names of some of the places they passed from listening to records and playing in the band. Now he was physically right there.

Once over the Texas-New Mexico state line, they motored through Tucumcari, Albuquerque, Gallup, and into Arizona. From that point on, the trip followed the lyrics to a song Ray knew from his Gulliver days called "Route 66." The classic tune was essentially a musical roadmap to follow if you had the means to "motor west" and where you could "get your kicks." The growing popularity of automobiles and the introduction of an interstate highway system were passports to a new mode of travel and exploration. Folks saw California as a land of unlimited opportunity where they could create their personal shangri-la. The newly-constructed U.S Route 66 literally paved the way, and was beginning to play a significant role in the country's transportation history.

The song's 1,200 mile trip to motor west went like this:

"...go down from St. Louis
To Joplin, Missouri
Oklahoma City, she looks so pretty
You'll see Amarillo
Gallup, New Mexico
Flagstaff, Arizona
Don't forget Winona

Kingman, Barstow, San Bernardino
Get your kicks
On Route 66..."

They spent the night in a parking lot in the high desert town of Kingman, Arizona where the temperature climbs to 120 degrees during the day and falls to 40 degrees at night. Dupree remarked that Texans call that a long thermometer. He said during the winter months, it can drop into the 20s at night and he's seen it snow there occasionally. That flew in the face of Ray's perception of the desert, which was basically an endless, barren landscape, oppressive heat, and bone dry, with vultures circling overhead. In his wildest dreams, Ray never thought the desert's harsh and unforgiving veneer could give way to such indescribable beauty if one took the time to look deeply enough. It's a queer yet magnificent marriage between the imposing grandeur of towering mountains and the lowly simplicity of scrubby, hardscrabble desert. The extreme paradox these polar opposites create is what makes their marriage so magnificent and enduring. It proved that opposites do attract.

First up for the day was Barstow, just a smidgeon over the California-Arizona border, and then they'd put the hammer down for the final hitch through San Bernardino and into Los Angeles. It finally hit Ray like a ton of bricks; no longer was he singing "California, here I come." Now, it was California, here I am. He could taste it.

CHAPTER FIFTEEN

California's Cajon Pass descends steeply from the high desert at an elevation of 4,500 feet above sea level into the rugged San Bernardino Mountain range below. Dupree said the combination of the truck's tonnage, steadily increasing downhill speed, and a sharp, miles-long curve, can be awfully nerve-wracking, particularly in bad weather. Maintaining control of his rig required his full attention behind the wheel. His focus had to be not only on his own driving, but on all the other truckers ahead and on each side who could lose control of their rigs and jacknife at any moment.

The landscape changed dramatically as soon as they reached "San Berdoo," as Dupree called it, accentuated by giant 40-foot tall palm trees all in a row along the highway. With their fronds swaying so gracefully in the breeze, they appeared to be waving a friendly hello. After the blinding assault on their eyes from driving through the stifling desert heat, the city's attractive landscaping was a welcome sight. And bright sunshine and 75 degrees with a slightl breeze was a welcome relief from the relentless heat.

Traffic was bumper-to-bumper as the Freightliner approached downtown Los Angeles, which marked the end of the line for Ray. Driving the big rig at a crawl gave Dupree quite a workout from the non-stop clutching, gear shifting, and braking every 10 seconds or so. Ray could see tiny beads of sweat forming on his forehead as he inched his way to the off-ramp and finally made it to Union Station. Ray's final, final leg was catching a bus to Oceanside, where his sister and brother-in-law were expected to meet him.

Dupree was on the clock, so he didn't have much time for long goodbyes. Neither did Ray because he knew he'd start crying and didn't want to end the trip that way. Dupree pulled out a $20 bill and stuffed it in Ray's shirt pocket for the bus fare and a burger. They looked at each other and, without exchanging words, telepathically conveyed how grateful they were for the blood they share as relatives that spills over into the love they share as long-time friends, even after all the years that passed. This was a solemn moment in time they'd cherish for eternity.

Dupree pulled out and saluted Ray with two final blasts on his horn and disappeared into the line of traffic exiting the station. Ray stood there and once again got that feeling of being all alone, much like he did when his parents dropped him at school and took off for the races. He bought a one-way ticket to Oceanside, downed a couple of burgers and a chocolate shake, and parked himself on a huge wooden bench until his scheduled departure time.

After boarding, he took a window seat, sat back, and watched the seaside show: surfers paddling out and catching waves, thousands upon thousands of tanned bodies lying on the beach. Tiny tots filling their buckets and building sandcastles. And there was a special treat: a pod of dolphins just offshore heading south. That was a first for him.

Ray felt the excitement building in his gut and pounding in his heart. His thoughts bounced around in his head like pinballs, but it was imperative that he keep any fear and doubt from creeping in and torpedoing everything he just sacrificed and suffered for in order to make this move.

When he stepped off the bus, he looked for a familiar face but didn't see anyone he recognized. Perhaps he took the wrong bus or got off at the wrong stop. He was about to ask someone for help when he heard a voice call out, "Ray-Ray!"

He spun around to locate the source. "Ray, we're over here!"

Ray quickly scanned the crowd and picked out Bonnie Lee's smiling face and her frantically waving arms. They wrapped their arms around each other for a good minute, and smiled and sobbed and then laughed and sobbed again.

"Ray-Ray, I want to introduce you to my husband, ValMor," she announced, looking toward the gentleman standing next to her whom Ray failed to notice. He didn't make the connection that they were together.

"I'm ValMor Stiles, it's a pleasure to meet you," he said with a booming voice while extending a massive hand to shake.

With a furrowed brow, eyes wide and mouth agape, Ray muttered a weak "Hi," limply shook his hand, and just stood and stared at him. ValMor broke into an ear-to-ear smile, flashing a gorgeous set of beautifully straight, bright white teeth that looked as if he'd swallowed a piano. He saw that Ray was suffering from a mild case of aftershock. Bonnie-Lee knew her brother well and could read his body language. It was time to address the 800-pound elephant in the room.

She half-laughed and said, "Yes, Ray-Ray, my husband's black!"

CHAPTER SIXTEEN

Ray had his a-ha! moment when he connected the dots and finally realized that Val-Mor was the reason for Bonnie Lee suddenly disappearing from home in the middle of the night, with a person the family didn't know, running off to God knows where. He agreed that their stubborn, simple-minded parents would never understand or accept a black man in the family and would only make her life miserable. She made a bold and courageous decision that night to take full control of her life and her own destiny from that point on. Ray commended her and told her how proud he was that she first made herself happy this time instead of worrying about making Mom and Dad happy.

The three made their way to the parking lot and easily spotted Val-Mor's bright yellow Volkswagen van, which he dubbed "The Yellow Submarine." As a professed Beatles fan, Ray was familiar with the song and thought the handle was a little on the goofy side. Val-Mor and Bonnie Lee had their arms around one another and snuck in a kiss that Ray tried not to notice but caught out of the corner of his eye. However, he was hyper-aware of several people in the parking lot staring; some were mad dogging them, tsk-tsking them, shaking their heads disapprovingly, and mumbling something indecipherable under their breath.

It takes an awful lot of time and patience, Bonnie Lee admitted as they loaded into the van and pulled out of the bus station parking lot. Her voice resonated with notes of frustration and hurtfulness, taking care to avoid full-blown anger. At first, she found it infuriating and wanted to confront those who had the gall to judge her and the person with whom she chose to cherish and spend her life.

"People have no idea of the nasty insults complete strangers hurl at us," she lamented. "And the shaming and the judging we have to put up with... it's so intense, and ugly, and hurtful and even sad that people can feel that way. But you know what Ray, going through that just proved that when two people love one another, color don't matter. So, we try to stay focused on that and ignore their ignorance."

On the drive home, Ray sounded like an inquisitive three-year old child hounding them with questions. He wanted to hear more about how and where they met and then wound up in California. He was curious about living in Leucadia and what there was to see and do. It was non-stop the entire drive. Bonnie Lee said it was a long story and he would have to wait until they got home, a darling little bungalow tucked into a corner of Hygeia Avenue and within walking distance of the beach. Ray hopped out of the van and instantly felt a warm ocean breeze on his face, even though it was late at night. He smelled the heavy salt air and caught a whiff of a scent he couldn't identify, only because night blooming jasmine doesn't grow anywhere in New Jersey.

Over a bottle of red wine, Bonnie Lee described the first time she and Val-Mor had any contact as somewhat awkward and uncomfortable. She was living at home and working behind the counter at Freeman's Bakery in Plainfield, New Jersey, and Val-Mor was a customer she waited on a few times. He was on leave from the Marines for a month and came in every morning and bought a dozen black and whites, half-moon cookies. He tried to impress her by waxing poetically about the manner in which two starkly opposite colors coexist so wondrously on a shortbread cookie.

"Know what I see when I look at this cookie?" Val-Mor asked her. "You and me, baby!"

P.U. That line stunk, she thought to herself.

At first, Bonnie Lee thought Val-Mor was a blustery cuss with a lame pick-up line, but she failed to understand that he was using half-moon cookies as a metaphor to show how opposites do attract and can actually create a better version of themselves together. It was a subtle yet clever show of his romantic intentions. He found Bonnie Lee attractive, witty, and utterly charming.

Bonnie Lee began to see he was using this move as an ice-breaker, but as nice a man as he seemed, she wanted no part of him. She dated here and there but wasn't in a serious relationship and wasn't looking for one. After several breakups, she was enjoying the fact that she had no attachments at the moment. The interracial aspect was also an issue that she could do without, not because of any prejudices she held, but instead having to deal with the destructive attacks and jaded comments from family, friends, and strangers.

Before she knew it, she surrendered to Val-Mor's steady advances and fell hard for him. In just a month's time, she felt certain enough that Val-Mor was the one she wanted to spend eternity with; she believed he was sent to cross her path, win her over, and help her begin a life where she's finally in charge and making the decisions rather than cow-towing to everyone else. Plus, she loved his name. Val-Mor was a USMC Gunnery

Sergeant assigned to Paris Island Marine Corps base in South Carolina, and the couple moved to southern California about two years ago after he was transferred to Camp Pendleton.

"And Mom and Dad still don't know! That's incredible," Ray exclaimed. "Well, good on you guys. Looks like you're very happy and enjoying your new life. So, here's to you! Salud!" They all raised their glasses and toasted to health, happiness, and new horizons.

Ray wasted no time getting out of the house to explore Leucadia and the surrounding towns using Val-Mor's bicycle. High up on the nearby bluffs that overlook the Pacific Ocean, he noticed a huge white mansion that featured minarets and a gold-domed roof, and right next to it was a lush meditation garden with koi ponds and the most exotic flora he'd ever seen. After speaking with an elderly man who had been meditating, Ray was told these magnificent gardens were owned and maintained by the Self-Realization Fellowship. The man who owned the mansion on the bluffs was Paramahansa Yogananda, a maharishi yogi and the founder of SRF, which is a retreat and spiritual learning center for the study of transcendental meditation. Ray thought back to the rooftop gardens he tended at Odyssey House and these were on an entirely different level. He would definitely be returning.

On the way home, Ray pedaled past a funky, bright yellow, Victorian-style-house-turned-cafe when the aroma of freshly roasted coffee beans forced him to make a U-turn and check the place out. He sat at a table sipping a coffee and surveying the room when a few surfers pulled up chairs and sat down at a nearby table. They all noticed each other at the same time and exchanged hellos. The small talk turned to lengthier conversations involving Ray's decision to move cross country and basically start his life over at 36 years old. Now feeling more comfortable, Ray started peppering them with questions and picking their brains about the place he chose to begin his life anew.

They told Ray he might hear the locals referring to Leucadia by its quirky nickname. Seems the quiet beach town had earned a reputation as the go-to place to score quaaludes, and from there, the ingenious new name "Quaaludia" was born. Ray found the name clever and amusing. Another customer sitting nearby chimed in, explaining the word "leucadia" has a couple of different origins and translations. In Greek, leucadia translates to "place of refuge, pure, bright;" in Spanish, it's used to describe objects "of splendid brightness." That description sounded mighty encouraging to Ray, and he was ready for some brightness after the onslaught of gloom that pervaded his life of late.

Ray mentioned that he was living temporarily with his sister and brother-in-law, and planned to start looking for a job right away. He needed to make some money and find his own place to settle. One guy in the group who introduced himself as Drew, told Ray that his father owned a landscaping business and was looking to hire a helper. He gave Ray the phone number and recommended that he call as soon as he could.

Ray took Drew's advice and phoned Drew's father, Earl, the minute he arrived back at the bungalow. They met the next day for an introduction and interview, and both felt an instant connection. Ray was hired as a laborer, and would be digging holes, planting and pruning trees, maintaining lawns and gardens, mixing mortar for the retaining walls they designed, and supplying them with the bricks and cement block needed for construction of any landscaping features. Earl confessed it was strenuous but physically rewarding work, and judging by Ray's size and fit appearance, thought he was capable of handling it.

Ray showed up early on his first day and got a quick lesson and demonstration from Drew on the use of a pole saw. They loaded up the truck and headed for their first job of the day a short distance away. When they arrived, Ray was instructed to take care of trimming all of the homeowner's palm trees. Some of these trees were 30 feet tall, and had pale yellow, dried-out fronds still attached and hung limply from the trunk, and were long overdue for pruning. Ray was jazzed about being productive again, doing work he enjoyed, and feeling comfortable outdoors in his element.

His first few attempts with the tool were clumsy, and got a few belly laughs from Drew and Earl. He soon got the hang of it and spent the entire morning pruning and trimming. They broke for lunch and sat in the shade munching on a tuna fish sandwich and washing it down with an iced tea. Earl asked Ray if he had any hobbies or interests, and he immediately answered that he played guitar. Earl also played guitar and sang and had regular gigs with a bit of a local following. He suggested they kick it around some evening and Ray enthusiastically agreed.

They jammed three or four times, and the vibe was strong. Ray was adding a lot to Earl's sound, and he liked what he was hearing. He invited Ray to back him up for his next gig at a local vegetarian cafe and juice bar called The Shepherd. Ray couldn't believe he was getting a second chance to play live music again.

With Ray's addition, Earl noticed a difference in the way the audience responded to this bigger sound and more refined performance. Through word of mouth, his following grew larger and regularly packed the place every time they played, which greatly pleased the owner and guaranteed them steady work. Earl hired him for several other regular jobs and soon Ray was playing out three nights a week. Along with a day job, he was putting a lot of hours into his work and getting ever closer toward his goal of having his own place. Playing live music well into the night and getting home late, he was concerned that he wasn't getting enough sleep in order to be physically prepared for the next day's work.

Ray overslept one morning and showed up a few minutes late for work. Earl told him not to make a habit of it but understood at the same time that Ray was burning the candle at both ends and doing a good job at both. They loaded up and drove to a job at a hoity-toity country club in nearby Rancho Bernardo, where the members dress in all white and play tennis and outdoor shuffleboard all day. Ray had trimming and pruning duty after he loaded three wheelbarrows full of bricks and set them up for Earl and Drew.

He grabbed the pole saw and began routinely pruning the lower fronds of a monster queen palm. His mind drifted to his gig the previous night and some of the attractive ladies he met. He was feeling content with his new life so far and pleased with the fact that he had money in his pocket with two sources of income from his favorite pursuits. He was finally thinking he was in pretty good shape, mentally, physically, and emotionally.

Without warning, the pruning tool snapped backward and the force knocked the pole saw out of Ray's hands. He saw it flying toward him and instinctively raised his right hand to protect his face. When he felt the impact on his hand, he looked down in shock and horror to see three of his fingers hanging by sinewy threads, and blood pumping out of a severed vein with each beat of his heart. He was too much in the state of shock to even let out a scream.

Earl and Drew rushed over to him, pulled off their t-shirts, and wrapped them around his mangled hand to control the bleeding. They jumped in the truck and drove like jehu to the nearest emergency room, where a team of doctors and surgeons were already waiting to operate. Ray was delirious from the excruciating pain, spouting gibberish, and fading in and out of consciousness. Earl and Drew stood stone-like outside the ER entrance, shirtless and covered in Ray's blood, trying to wrap their heads around the horrific event they just witnessed. With their adrenaline pumping and having to think and act fast, they hadn't yet fully grasped, until that moment, the severity of Ray's injury and the uncertain future that lay ahead. He may never work again, and even more tragically, he may never play the guitar again.

It was more than obvious the cruelty of Murphy's Law knew no bounds.

CHAPTER SEVENTEEN

Ray was literally and figuratively beside himself. Actually, it was more like he was above himself. A wispy cloud floated by near the ceiling and Ray sat Indian-style on it, gazing down confusedly at himself lying in a hospital bed. He was asleep and heavily sedated, and his bandaged hand was as big as a catcher's mitt. The Ray up on the cloud wondered if the pitiful sight below him was an acid flashback, or if he died and was having an out of body experience. Or was this simply an outlandish dream sequence where his spirit levitated above the bed and floated around on a puffy white cloud.

The door blew wide open with what felt like hurricane-strength gusts of wind and suddenly the room was awash in a spectacular radiance. It was indescribably brilliant, but at the same time it emitted a soft edge and a comforting warmth that settled over Ray's entire body like a blanket. Then, as quickly as the bizarre incident began, it was over. Ray thought to himself, "Where did all of that come from?"

"I commanded it," Ray heard a powerful voice reply from out of nowhere. Was he hearing voices now?

He turned his head to the left and there was his Lord and savior, Jesus Christ, sharing the cloud with him. In the flesh, or so it seemed. Now Ray was positive he was dead, and Jesus had come to render judgement on his life. He fully believed this was the moment he had been preparing for most of his life: the honor and privilege of barely slithering through the Kingdom's narrow gate and on to his eternal reward.

"Raymond, do not have any fear," He told him. "You aren't going to die. I won't let you. You're needed to help me carry out a very important mission. I chose you because you've suffered great loss, yet you stayed resilient. You kept your faith in me and sought my help. Well, here I am. I have finally come to answer your prayers and for you to answer mine."

"Is this a dream, Lord, or is this really happening?" Ray asked.

"Yes, you are part of a dream, my dream, and yes, my apparition and my requests are quite real. I want you to keep your eyes and ears wide open and you will learn all you need to know for you to see that my will is done."

"What is it you want me to do?"

Jesus then struck a more serious tone and spoke to Ray about too many people abusing drugs to treat their pain and illness or help them forget about their problems. They aren't respecting their bodies and minds as the Father intended. They search for quick fixes and instant gratification from powders and pills when all they really need to heal can be found all around them. They just have to open their eyes and see.

"In my name, Raymond, I want you to build for me the great Gardens of Aloe Vera, with the magnificence of the Garden of Eden and the Hanging Gardens of Babylon. It will be a sacred site that I have chosen to bring health and wellness to all. Their souls will be blessed by me and they will heal themselves with the natural remedies that were created by my

Father for that very purpose. I will teach you how, and show you the way, and then you will have to do the same for others and show them the way."

Jesus gently placed his hand on Ray's shoulder and said He would show him what He had in mind. Again, a blaze of light saturated the room and when Ray could see again, he found himself mysteriously teleported to the summit of a granite-faced mountain in a place he had never seen before. He gazed down at the expansive desert floor below him and marveled at the masterpiece of nature that lay before his eyes. Never in his wildest dreams could he have imagined any garden as stunning.

He told Ray that His great gardens will be a crown jewel in the desert, a thriving, life-giving oasis specially chosen and lovingly placed here by his Father's hand. It was His gift to any who possessed the wisdom to appreciate the powers of natural healing.

"I am giving you a photographic memory so that you capture every detail. It must be exactly as you see it here, so pay careful attention and do not take shortcuts or make any decisions on your own. Do not make the same mistake that Adam and Eve did, " Christ joked.

Together they scanned the landscape with Jesus pointing out rows upon rows of aloes of every variety, shape and size that seemed to stretch all the way to infinity. He envisioned a viscous, lava-like flow of aloe gel snaking lazily through the gardens, where bathers line up on the banks to dip in their hands and toes for a dose of the healing gel which they rubbed over their entire bodies. All along the river, there were groves of trees bursting with fruits, fields full of every imaginable vegetable, herb gardens, poppy fields, orchids, lavender, jasmine, jades, and rare topiary and ornamentals he never knew existed.

He explained to Ray that The Father chose the location because of its natural hot springs and sulphur springs that people can soak in and use the powers of nature to restore energy by ridding their bodies of harmful, debilitating toxins.

"Take a look over there at that humongous aloe sculpture and fountain, Raymond. I'd like that to be the showpiece of the gardens and the new community that surrounds it. It will become a destination, a landmark dedicated to the preservation of holistic healing, with therapeutics generously provided by Mother Nature. People will make pilgrimages to seek it out."

He pointed to an immense commercial growing operation and production facility where busy workers chopped, blended, processed and packaged tons of harvested aloes on assembly lines.

"Right there is the engine that makes all of this work," He told Ray. People were lined up at an aloe juice bar sampling blended fruits and vegetables they picked themselves from the gardens right in front of them. There was a yoga class, saunas, a salt water swimming pool, and meditation gardens. Children playfully navigated a labyrinth made of thick hedgerows and tried to make their way through a corn maze.

Ray looked at Jesus incredulously and asked, "You really believe I can do this, Lord?"

He was quickly reminded of Christ's omniscience.

"Raymond, I know you can do this, and you will. When you prayed, you told me you'd do anything I asked of you. My son, you must show the same faith you had when you were overwhelmed with your many trials and tribulations. You believed I was the only way out of your misery and suffering. Only through me, with me, and in me did you find the will to keep going. Continue using that as your guide and I will see that you are rewarded for placing your hope and faith in me."

Ray looked up and saw heavy, dark clouds roll in and drape the mountain top. The warmth he experienced before disappeared and he suddenly felt a chill. He looked over where Christ stood and was shocked to find He was gone. All of a sudden, it was like watching a solar eclipse and the world went black.

When Ray woke up a short time later, he had no idea where he was or how he got there. He looked at his heavily wrapped hand but hadn't been told yet that the index, middle and ring fingers on his right hand couldn't be reattached and had to be amputated. His thumb and pinky finger were all that was left. From then on, rather than wallow in pity over his disability, he could make it a positive by using it as a reminder to always "hang loose."

Through his morphine-induced haze, Ray was trying his hardest to figure out whether he was dead in his bed awaiting his fate, or just waking up groggy as all get out from some drug-induced wild and crazy dream. As soon as his hand started throbbing, he knew it was neither. This was real. Scary.

CHAPTER EIGHTEEN

How life can change with a snap of the fingers. In an instant, Ray went from a happy, able-bodied man working two jobs, playing music, and living a block from the beach to a disabled, jobless, and depressed walking waste of time. His life was now a torturous cycle of constant wound care, skin grafts, and physical therapy, all with a heavy dose of painkillers.

Ray had nothing but time on his hands, but had nowhere to go and nothing constructive to do. He could ride the bike one-handed so he started making it a part of his daily routine. Cruising around the neighborhood, he noticed a group of people on the beach playing guitars and singing, so he approached them and asked whether they would mind if he joined in. They passed around a few joints and a bottle of Boone's Farm Apple Wine, and for a couple of hours, Ray was distracted from his miserable life.

One of the guys playing guitar named Bruce introduced Ray to the group, each of whom welcomed him and made him feel comfortable. They went around the circle and introduced themselves. There was Cat, his girlfriend Krystal, Little Tree, Barefoot Bill, Snake Eyed Jake, and Uncle Paint. A sunburned, pony-tailed stoner named Breeze offered him a packet of Charms candy, compliments of the factory where he worked the overnight shift as a supervisor on the packaging line. Jake pumped gas at a local Hess station, where they all hung out and referred to as the Space Station.

He could be out there himself at times, but Ray thought these people were on a completely different planet. Nonetheless, he had nobody to hang out with and he found them twisted but mildly amusing, so he started spending a lot of time with this pack of obvious miscreants. Meanwhile, he began strumming his guitar a little after Bruce came up with the idea of using a thumb pick. Brilliant.

These characters lived commune-style in a slovenly and long-neglected geodesic dome. The only furniture in the place was a bean bag chair and a picnic table in the kitchen. No beds; they all slept on the floor. When they bathed, they did so outside in rainwater that collected in an old porcelain bathtub. Bruce worked a few hours a week at an organic produce market and often brought home anything that was too old or rotten to sell and destined for the dumpster. Ray was eventually invited over to jam with them and was blown away by the scene. Inside, the musicians and a couple of other stragglers sat on the floor and ran through a half-dozen, half-assed attempts at covering the classic jazz tune by the great Dave Brubeck titled, "Take Five." So after about 20 minutes, everybody followed Brubeck's advice.

A few days later, Ray took the liberty of inviting a bunch of them over to jam at the Hygeia Avenue house where he was living. Someone in the group passed a joint around that Ray thought tasted weird, like spearmint. Minutes later, completely dazed and practically immobile, Ray felt an elbow in his ribs. It was Jackie the uke player.

"Hey man, I think we just got dusted," she quietly told him. The joint he smoked wasn't even real weed. It was rolled up spearmint leaves sprinkled with Angel Dust.

Conscious but virtually incapacitated, they all lost track of time and didn't clear out before Bonnie Lee arrived home from work. She exploded on Ray and ordered the "low lifes" out of her home and warned them to never darken her door again.

"That's it, Ray. I've lost my patience with you and so has Val-Mor. You're gonna' have to go," she said sternly. "You've taken advantage of our kindness and now you disrespected our home by inviting those strangers here. You had no regard whatsoever for our privacy or security. I don't know them and what they might be capable of doing, and neither do you."

Ray sheepishly apologized and blamed part of his poor judgment on the painkillers, to which he was now addicted. They both agreed to a cooling-off period, with Bonnie Lee suggesting Ray go and live with them in that dome. He'd at least have a roof over his head and food to eat.

Ray packed his bag and, as he left, told his sister again how sorry and ashamed he was, and how much he appreciated everything she and her husband did for him. He promised he would do his best to earn back their respect.

On his way to the dome to ask if he could crash there for a few days, he ran into Barefoot Bill, who was, of course, pounding the pavement with no socks or shoes on his gnarly looking feet. His eyes were practically bugging out through his wire-rimmed glasses, and Ray could see that both he and the dirty clothes he was wearing needed a thorough cleaning. As Bill spoke, excess saliva pooled in the corners of his mouth, and he looked and sounded like he was in another world. That's because he was – his own. He scarcely stopped talking long enough for Ray to ask for his permission, and after boiling down his long-winded, meandering reply, he came to the conclusion that Bill was okay with him staying there temporarily.

When Ray walked toward the dome, he saw the group already had a campfire going and were cooking hot dogs on a stick.

"Find yourself a nice long, green branch and have a pooch," Jackie said with a mouthful of hot dog and bun. Ray liked her right away because she was a proud lifetime stoner, good-natured, and she played an awesome jazz ukulele. Ray was starved and didn't hesitate to accept her offer. As they sat around and chomped on fire-roasted wieners on a stick, Ray asked about some of their more unusual nicknames, like Uncle Paint, who was expected to join them shortly.

"From what he told me, he was a big huffer in high school," Cat confided. Ray wasn't familiar with that word and asked what it meant.

"He liked to get high sniffing paint," Cat said. "Fill a big baggie with regular old house paint, stick his face in the bag, and start huffing, you know breathing in and out real fast to take in the fumes. Some crazy stuff there. He even had a favorite color paint called Minty Flinty. He said it smelled good."

Everyone roared and then fell silent, allowing the crackling fire to cast its mesmerizing spell. Cat spoke up and revealed he got his name as a young boy when his cat-like behaviors caught his parents' attention. They said he was quick on his feet, crafty, agile, and, at times, detached or aloof.

Ray then turned and looked at Little Tree.

"Well, I may not look it right now with my long hair and scraggly beard, but I am a proud Native American and member of the Paiute

Tribe of Bishop. My given family name is LittleTree and my first name is actually WhiteClaw. But nobody calls me that, so they wound up calling me by my family name."

Ray was utterly transfixed. LIttle Tree explained the name fit perfectly because when he was a young boy, his mother pointed out that he often reminded her of a lone Bristlecone pine tree on the reservation. Short and stunted from battling the extreme elements of the high desert, it had a noticeably thick trunk with a couple of scrawny branches for arms. As petrified and deformed as it was, she saw its inherent beauty and resilience, and gazing at it in the distance became part of her everyday life.

Ray heard some shouting and slamming doors from inside the dome that sounded like Cat and Krystal having a big time argument. Ray didn't want to listen to that noise, so he decided to leave and walked to the beach to sit and think. It was low tide, the waves were quiet little ankle slappers, and a nearly full moon was rising and reflecting on the ocean. It was enough to lull Ray into a blissful catnap after which he headed back to the dome.

When he rounded the corner of the block, he saw a flood of flashing red lights, hoses lying all over the street, and billows of acrid smoke choking out the salty night air. Ray asked one of the firefighters what was happening.

"Some freak got into a scrape with his dingbat girlfriend and decided to get revenge with a Molotov cocktail," shouted the fireman over the radio chatter. "I guess that was his idea of celebrating Happy Hour."

Ray knew instantly the "freak" person of interest had to be Cat. He stood in the middle of the street, staring in disbelief at the height of the flames shooting out of that tiny tinderbox and lighting up the night sky. His temporary home was no more and his guitar– really his only possession in the world besides the clothes on his back – was more than likely vaporized in the spectacular blaze right in front of him. That song about having nothing but bad luck started playing in his head again, until a shadowy figure emerged from a curtain of smoke holding a ukulele in one hand and Ray's unblemished guitar in the other.

CHAPTER NINETEEN

Once again, Bonnie Lee came to the rescue. When she learned of Ray's misfortunes and knew there was no one he could turn to, she accepted his apology and agreed to take him back and allow him to live in the Hygeia house, but under strict, zero-tolerance rules and restrictions. She genuinely wanted to see him get back on his feet and become happy and productive again, despite his disability. He had to figure out how he was going to live his life missing three fingers, and as difficult as that would be, it wasn't the end of the world in her mind.

Bonnie Lee's job in the county's social services agency required her at times to work with counterparts in other departments, including one that assisted low-income clients with finding affordable housing. She heard through the grapevine that the county wanted to dispose of a number of used trailers in its inventory and was selling them at well below market price. She could loan Ray the money, get him signed up for disability so he'd have some income to pay her back over time, and give him a hand up to kickstart his life. After all, he'd suffered more than his fair share of adversity in his life, and as his big sister, her heart held a special place for him.

Together, they visited several "coaches" that were on the county's inventory list, but there was only one that Ray found appealing enough to consider. It was in a trailer court called The Riviera, which was close to Bonnie Lee's place, plus the lot was nicely landscaped with a small garden and young fruit trees. The coach needed a new floor and bathroom plumbing, but they made an offer nonetheless, and it was accepted. Thanks to Bonnie Lee's big heart, Ray once again had a roof over his head, however there was plenty of work to do before it was a place he could realistically call home.

Ray spent the first couple of months introducing himself to neighbors and greeting passersby as they went about their everyday business in the park. That could mean doing laundry, taking a dip in the swimming pool, or taking the garbage to the dumpster, which happened to be a stone's throw away and visible from his galley window. Almost immediately, he noticed a few characters that stood out from the rest of the trailer park denizens, an assortment of working class heroes, retirees, hippies, surfers, alcoholics and drug addicts. Odds were pretty good there was a criminal or three on the lam living among them.

There were a couple of residents Ray noticed who were obviously mentally disabled. One of them was called Crazy George, and he would simply ride through the park on his bike all day long, smiling at everyone he saw but never speaking a word. The scuttlebutt was that he lived with his mother and she was his caregiver. Ray smiled and waved to George as he pedaled by everyday, but only got a smile back and no return wave. George always kept both hands on the handlebars. Another soul named Morris gave names to the trees in the trailer park. Among the names were Do-Chokey, 99-999, and Teddy Dagwagwa.

A wild-eyed hippie chick wearing an ankle-length denim skirt, a tie-dyed tee shirt and Birkenstocks on her feet, was another trailer rat Ray saw most every day. She made her rounds on foot, right past Ray's place, and almost always at the same time. He decided he'd go out of his way to be friendly, even though he heard she was a tweaker and her behavior could be bizarre and unpredictable, especially under the influence.

"Hey there, my name's Ray! I just moved in! Who are you?"

The woman kept her head down and completely ignored Ray's greeting, like he was invisible. She was focused on her technique, pumping her arms up and down like pistons, and rhythmically moving her hips from side to side with each frenzied stride. Her form looked good enough to compete for a spot on the US Race Walking Team. Ray wasn't sure if she heard him or if she was thoroughly engrossed in her own world. One thing was for sure: she moved fast.

Hence, her handle "Speedy." It was wisely chosen because it killed two birds with one stone. She was lightning fast on her feet as well as a world-class meth head. No one knew what she did for a living, if anything, and assumed she was on either welfare or disability because it seemed she would speed walk day and night, and couldn't do that if she held a real job.

Where there's such a melange of extraordinary characters there's sure to be a fair share of scuttlebutt, postulations, and dirty laundry tossed about. And there was no better place to air it all out than the park's laundromat. Ray quickly learned a lot about life in a trailer park by acting oblivious or disinterested, but tuning in to the different conversations taking place simultaneously. There was never any proof offered for confirmation, but there were plenty of opinions ricocheting off the walls that were clearly audible above the sounds of the busy washing machines and dryers.

"She was a hooker who worked out of her coach." "She was a Tarot card and palm reader." "She cooked meth in her bathtub to support her real calling, which was to follow the Grateful Dead around on their tours." She supposedly rode around in a VW van with some guy called "Space Dog," also a perfect moniker for someone who looked perpetually spaced out and dirty as a stray dog.

Of course, not one of them ever actually talked to Speedy and got the real skinny on her since she simply ignored any attempt at conversation. And so the rumors swirled, and like the infamous telephone game, they got juicier each time they were retold. In the process, the character and reputation of a woman to whom they never spoke, and whose real name they don't know, was besmirched and destroyed over cruel gossip and speculation. But it sure did liven up everybody's laundry day.

Ray started loading his clothes into a washing machine when a tall, slender, shirtless young man wearing tightly-fitting cut-offs and flip flops walked directly toward him and plopped his laundry bag on the machine right next to Ray's, even though there were plenty of other machines available.

"Why, hello there, you must be new here," came a soft, effeminate-sounding voice out of a mouth that instantly broke into a mile wide smile. The man extended his hand for Ray to shake while introducing himself as Danny. He opened the lid of the machine and began loading his clothes and detergent. While he was pumping quarters into the coin slot, he started telling Ray that he goes to the pool to suntan every afternoon around 2 in case he ever wanted to join him. Then he casually added in a hushed tone, "There's never anyone there, so we'd have the place all to ourselves," he said, followed by wink and a grin.

Those words caught Ray completely off guard. How does he respond to that? Does he go off on this guy, nip this in the bud right here and now, or politely decline the invitation, explaining he's busy working during the day and doesn't have time for sunbathing. Only that would be just kicking the can down the road. Sooner or later he would have to face telling Danny that he wouldn't mind becoming friends, but the truth is he didn't have any interest in having a romantic experience with him or any other man.

"No offense, Danny, and I suppose I should be flattered, but for me personally, there could never be anything that replaces the love between a man and a woman," Ray said.

"Okay, but if you ever change your mind, and you feel like taking a walk on the wild side, you be sure to call me first, hear?" Danny shot back, and then blew Ray a kiss as he strutted away.

That was a walk Ray had zero interest in taking, and nothing anyone could say or do would ever change his mind.

CHAPTER TWENTY

Walking back home, Ray noticed a large green box truck parked next to his coach and two Mexican men who appeared to be making a delivery. He couldn't recall ordering any gardening or landscaping supplies recently, and as he got closer, he saw the men were unloading these enormous, gorgeously shaped, picture-perfect *aloe vera barbadensis* plants. They were the cream of the crop in the aloe world.

"Hey, are you guys sure you have the right place? I never ordered these plants," Ray told them. They explained they had instructions from their boss to pick out 50 of the best looking barbadensis plants and deliver them here to this address. They confirmed his coach number 51.

"I don't have the money to pay for all of this," Ray replied in a mild panic. He was told there was no payment due. When Ray asked who the customer was who placed the order and gave them those instructions, they showed him a paper with the customer's name listed only as AG.

Ray stood there in disbelief as the men carried the aloes and carefully placed them in rows. He literally was watching his garden grow before his very eyes. He wondered who in the world could have done such a thing, and why? No one that he could think of in the park had shown any real interest in his meager little plot of a garden before this aloe windfall, nor would they have the funds to cover the exorbitant cost. He didn't know anybody with those initials. It was an enigma inside a mystery wrapped up in a riddle, but far be it from Ray to look this gift horse in the mouth. He could easily attest to the fact that life certainly can be full of surprises – some good, some bad –, but this was one for the books.

In the blink of an eye, Ray owned a considerable supply of the biggest, plumpest, healthiest aloes he'd ever seen. He began juicing the gel-packed spears with fresh-picked fruit from the trees growing right there in his garden; a veritable smorgasbord featuring apples, oranges, pears, plums, apricots, lemons and limes. Unbelievably, there was even a banana tree. He'd never seen a real, live banana tree before. He quickly found that juicing was a delightfully healthy and delicious way to start his day, particularly when combined with a couple of tokes on his hash pipe to set his head straight and put him in the proper frame of mind for digging his hands in the dirt.

Word traveled like wildfire about this new kid in town who turned a neglected, overgrown eyesore into a prize-winning garden that could grow virtually everything a person would need to stay alive indefinitely. People around the park took notice of Ray's expanding "garden of sustainability" as he referred to it, plus his seemingly bottomless supply of positive energy and enthusiasm for the work he did each day. They were full of questions and Ray was happy to answer, and he often wound up talking to them for hours. The scene resembled an event from the Bible and Jesus Christ's Sermon on the Mount. Ray's garden became somewhat of an in-park attraction, and folks started including it as a point of interest on their evening constitutionals. Before long, Ray had a half-dozen requests to design and build one just like his.

Ray didn't consider himself an expert in the landscape design field by any stretch of the imagination, but he now felt confident that he knew just enough to fake it. He picked up invaluable growing and design knowledge and experience from Dr. Judianne during his time working in the rooftop greenhouse. She showed him how to create a simple, functional, drought-resistant, and sustainable garden, using a variety of aloe veras and succulents as the focal point. The aloes are surrounded by an assortment of fruit trees, and a dedicated space for growing vegetables and herbs. She taught him about the importance of composting and mulching for a nutrient-rich soil that provides the perfect home for the earthworms so they can do what they do best: poop world-class fertilizer.

After seeing folks' interest and an immediate demand, Ray talked Bonnie Lee into co-signing a car loan and he purchased a neighbor's low-mileage, maroon 1979 Toyota stake-bed truck, and some basic tools and pieces of equipment he needed to take his home show on the road. His sister hand-painted two placards - one for each side of the bed – with a stylized aloe vera plant and the name Ray chose for his budding business: Aloe Age. He was proclaiming the dawn of the aloe age and he didn't even know it. It just sounded right.

CHAPTER TWENTY-ONE

After a particularly long, hot, arduous day of work, Ray settled back on his patio swing and devoured a carne asada burrito and a plate of rice and beans for a late *al fresco* dinner. He cracked open a cold Tecate, took a giant swallow, then picked up his acoustic guitar. He started riffing and strumming random chords, still working on his dexterity and technique since losing his fingers. He began playing an original tune he wrote years ago with a musician friend when he spotted what looked like the figure of a man who was standing nearby in the shadows and listening to him play. He finished the song and pretended no one was there watching and listening. Then from out of the darkness, Ray heard a deep, booming voice bellow, "Hey, sounded good, man. What's the name of that tune? I don't recognize it."

"Well, there's no way you would 'cuz it's an original that maybe three or four people on the entire planet have ever heard," Ray laughed. "But thanks. Care for a beer? Those are some deep pipes you got on you by the way."

The man thanked him for the compliment and the beer, and stayed a while to chit-chat about the heat and work and music and the collection of crazies they have to live with each day.

"Hey, I didn't get your name," Ray said to his guest. "I'm Ray."

"The name's Gabe. Pleased to meet you, Ray. I live in the end trailer," he replied. "Yeah, everyone around here knows your name, they call you the Aloe Man. Your garden is all the rage and the pride of the park."

Ray smiled and was pleased to hear that assessment of his work. He quickly changed the subject to ask if Gabe sang or played an instrument.

"Yeah, I play saxophone, but I'm not very good," he answered. "Haven't picked it up in a while."

Ray suggested he bring it over the next evening and they'd jam a few tunes before people started complaining about breaking the park's noise curfew.

"I'd love to hear you blow that horn. Hey, Gabriel! Come blow your horn! You probably get that a lot."

Late the next afternoon, Gabe showed up carrying a saxophone case, and behind him was a large bearded man wearing a red bandana. It was hard to believe, but it looked like he was pulling a wagon stacked with drums.

"Hey, Ray, I hope you don't mind that I brought along someone to help us keep time, plus he wouldn't take no for an answer. Say hello to…"

The guest visitor cut Gabe off mid-sentence and blurted out, "Just call me the wind, man… I blow in, do my thing, and then I blow out… that should tell you what I'm all about."

Ray and Gabe turned and looked at one another with raised eyebrows as they climbed the steps into the trailer. "I'll explain later," Gabe whispered.

"Should I just call you Mr. Wind or just plain Wind?" Ray asked with a chuckle while the mystery man set up his drum kit.

"Kind of a coinkydink; I was in a band years ago and my bandmates nicknamed me 'Windy.' They thought I was long-winded because I took forever to tell a story. I'd go off on tangents that were completely off-topic and never get to the point of the story."

"Call me Stickman, or Little Drummer Boy, or Funk Junkie, whatever you want. I answer to no one but myself. Anyway, we're burning daylight, so let's kick it, brother. That's what we're here for, 'aint it?" he scowled.

Gabe was a far better player than he said, and he added a lovely touch with his sax. Stickman laid down some nice grooves and became a little less hostile as the evening progressed. The trio improvised on classic songs that featured Gabe's smooth sax, like Van Morrison's jazzy "Moondance" and Sly and the Family Stone's funky "Everyday People." It had been ages since Ray played live with other musicians, and boy did it work wonders for his heart and soul. The music sounded pretty tight for three musicians who'd never been in a room together. Before the park's manager shut down the evening jam, a fun and receptive group of park residents gathered outside Ray's trailer and had themselves a spur of the moment listening party. They set up lawn chairs, packed coolers with beer, and some were even dancing in the street. It wasn't every day they got treated to free, live music and they were grateful for the evening's improvised entertainment.

As soon as they pulled the plug on the live music, Stickman broke down his kit and quickly departed with an abrupt *"Adios, amigos! Gracias, y Vaya con Dios!"* Like a summer thunderstorm, he blew in with a vengeance, kicked up a bit of a storm but didn't cause any serious damage, and then moved on through.

"Do you wanna' know who you just jammed with?" a grinning Gabe asked. He didn't give Ray time to answer.

"Ever heard of that band Canned Heat? They did "Goin' Up the Country," and "On the Road Again." That guy was their drummer. His name is Fito de la Parra! He played at Woodstock fer Chrissake!"

"That's so cool. I wish I'd known that; I would have been asking him a million questions," Ray said.

"The guy has played with some big name musicians," Gabe mentioned. He then reeled off a bunch of familiar names that Ray recognized, like The Platters, The Shirelles, T-Bone Walker, John Lee Hooker and Etta James.

Gabe explained that Fito is an extremely private person, and doesn't want people to know who he is, or was. He's also a paranoid schizophrenic who is supposed to be on medication, but he often blows them off and self-medicates. It looked to Gabe like he was off them at the moment and was acting a little nuttier than usual.

Ray asked how he knew the man.

"I lived next door to him growing up in the barrio in Long Beach, but I was really young when Canned Heat was just starting to make it, which really wasn't for very long. I used to listen to him practicing all the time and we became friends and jammed quite a bit."

Gabe said Fito drops in unannounced every once in a while, stays a couple of days, and then he's up and gone, blowing in the wind. He packs his drums into his VW van and drives around until he finds someone he can crash with and play some music, which is usually always Gabe.

Ray lit a joint and passed it to Gabe, who hesitated and admitted he hadn't smoked in a long time. Ray used the old "it's like riding a bicycle" line as a way of encouraging him to relax and indulge. After a few hits, they both settled back in their captain's chairs, pleasantly buzzed, and contentedly gazing up in complete silence at a perfectly full moon and a dazzling, star-filled sky.

Gabe finally broke the silence and asked Ray how he got into his line of work.

"This aloe thing just fell out of the sky and straight into my lap," he replied, referring to his new business. "See, a while back, I got busted for weed and did some time at a drug rehab in Harlem called Odyssey House. Then I was asked to become one of the resident counselors and worked there for six years. Lucky for me, I befriended the director, who was an avid gardener and had a rooftop greenhouse that she let me work in. She taught me so much and it was such good therapy for me. I didn't realize it at the time, but I do now."

Gabe said he honestly didn't know much about the aloe plant, other than it was applied topically to heal a wound or treat a sunburn. Ray responded that those were only the tip of the iceberg. He began rattling off a surprising number of benefits and uses of aloe vera, both from his own research and the knowledge he gained on the job as a gardener's helper.

Ray sounded almost encyclopedic, telling Gabe that his mentor, Dr. Denson-Gerber, called aloe vera the wonder plant and sang its praises as a natural healing agent for both inside and outside the body. It has an extra molecule of hydrogen peroxide, which gives it unique healing powers by way of strengthening the body's immune system. It's an antioxidant, which attacks free radicals that can cause oxidation; it's an anti-inflammatory, and a pain-relieving analgesic. It can be used as a laxative and has proven an effective treatment for acne, dry skin and wrinkles due to its rare collagen-synthesis properties. It's rich in Vitamins A, C, and E, and contains vital amino acids the body needs to function properly.

"Whoa, that was like listening to the Aloe Vera Medicine Show right there," Gabe joked. "That woulda' sold me. If you had a bottle of that magic elixir, I'd buy it on the spot."

Ray admitted that aloe vera was suddenly the focal point in his life and he actually had little to do with it. He wondered whether the planets aligned, or his moon was in Jupiter, or it was plain dumb luck. He told Gabe about his dream, in which Jesus personally instructed him to spread the Aloe Vera gospel worldwide, and use the gifts God created here on earth for natural healing of body and mind. By putting it in perspective for Gabe, Ray was beginning to see that his dream was in fact real; it was not a flashback or a figment of his imagination from the painkillers as he previously thought. Now, the task at hand was to start figuring out how to turn that dream into a reality, which would be no small task.

CHAPTER TWENTY-TWO

The hot, dry Santa Ana winds were already howling by noontime. A bunch of wildfires raged all night to the north and east of Ray's location and on that morning, the acrid smell of smoke was palpable. People complained about irritation in their eyes, nose, and throat. The thermometer in Ray's garden, in the shade, read a smidgeon over 100 degrees, and for most people, being outside even for a minute, was like standing in front of the door of a 400 degree oven with the door flung open. Not Ray, though. He loved the furious winds of change that blew in every year, carrying with them unbearable heat and bone dry humidity.

Normally, the westerly trade winds blow onshore and act like the world's largest air conditioner, keeping temperatures at a mild and comfortable 75 or so degrees at the beach, while it's a blazing 115 degrees in the desert just a hundred miles inland. In late summer and early fall when the Santa Anas are active, however, the wind directions get reversed. It becomes an offshore flow that originates in the desert and rages fiercely over the mountains and toward the coast, picking up speed and momentum along the way, carrying with it the desert's stifling heat.

Ray began his work day a little earlier than usual so he could lay low later and try his best to stay as cool as the center seed of a cucumber during the real heat of the day. He was on his hands and knees, pulling weeds from his aloe garden and removing the remnants of dead snails, when he noticed two feet standing beside him. He looked up but was blinded by the sun and couldn't make out who they belonged to.

"Hey, Aloe Man!" came the enthusiastic greeting from a voice he recognized as Gabe's.

"Thought you might want to take a break from this heat." He was holding two tall glasses of ice cold, hand-squeezed lemonade and a spleef. "I added some aloe, too!"

The fruit came from Ray's Meyer lemon tree, and the aloe vera gel from the gargantuan barbadensis plants that grew in his garden.

They took a seat on a bench in the shade and gulped down their drinks without speaking a word.

Ray seemed well-pleased that Gabe used the gifts from his garden so wisely, and as it turned out, so deliciously.

"That's lip-smacking good, right there" said Gabe, puckering his lips a few times.

"Nectar of the gods, right off the tree," Ray chimed in. "Man, those lemons sure are tasty."

The temperature was steadily rising, and it was getting too hot to work outside in the garden, so Ray called it a day. He stowed his tools and equipment in his shed, and invited Gabe inside where they could cool down and do some reasoning with the help of that spleef Gabe brought with him.

"Ray, I realize we haven't been friends and neighbors all that long, but in the time I've known you, I feel comfortable around you and talking to you, and I sort of get the feeling you have the same vibe," Gabe began. "So I want to talk to you about something really important."

"OK, Gabe, I'm all ears," he retorted. "What's on your mind?"

Gabe started by telling Ray that he recently lost his father, whose name coincidentally was Raymond. Raymond was a highly regarded chemist and geneticist who worked in R&D for a large pharmaceutical corporation. He developed and patented a number of breakthrough drugs and made a boatload in profits for his employer. He was rewarded handsomely for his work with shares of company stock, and became extremely wealthy from his investments. But that financial freedom and independence also came at a personal cost.

Raymond despised the rampant corruption, insatiable greed, and downright evil that he witnessed, and was forced to contend with, day after day. It was just as stunning as the astronomical number of human beings all over the world who suffered and died from the adverse effects of pharmaceuticals that were never sufficiently studied and were rushed to market. The tacit company line was always profits first, consumers last. And he felt like a hypocrite for having to toe that line to ensure his privileged livelihood.

Raymond soon saw a golden opportunity to make his next career move and decided to take his money and run away from big pharma as fast as his little feet could take him. He started a business that researched and developed all-natural healing remedies, exclusively using botanicals in place of the deleterious, highly toxic chemicals and compounds found in the products the pharmaceutical companies were constantly pushing. No matter the ailment, they've got the cure; just pop this pill and *abracadabra!* the pain magically vanishes. Then they have another pill to counter the side effects of the first pill, and on and on spins this wheel of misfortune. Their mission and vision was, simply, better living through chemistry.

Raymond amassed a mountain of research and developed an innovative organic product line of probiotics and other different types of herbal/ natural foods before eventually selling the start-up company for a tidy sum and a handsome profit. In pursuit of his personal happiness and well-being, he decided to take his years of R&D work to the next level and actually get his hands dirty. He was about to jump into a new horticulture business with both feet.

"He believed in using the God-given gifts our world offers us naturally, Gabe explained. "Our ancestors didn't have the luxury of taking a magic pill to manage their pain or cure a disease, so they discovered ways to treat illnesses and medicate with whatever was available around them. Dad wanted to see the entire world get off the medication merry-go-round and allow the body to heal itself naturally. But he didn't hide the fact that an ulterior motive was to crush the pharmaceutical companies financially and expose them for the frauds they were by showing people there were effective, renewable, sustainable, and affordable alternatives.

"Sorry to say he had a massive stroke and died right before he was about to set his plan in motion. But before he passed, he made me swear I would see it through and make sure all of his hard work wasn't in vain."

Gabe explained that right before his death, Raymond placed his many billions in a trust for him. He also purchased 400 acres in the southern Arizona desert that he planned to turn into a sprawling commercial farming operation and a massive production facility. His plant palette consisted of a variety of aloes, herbs, and drought-resistant succulents. He wanted more than anything to inform the world that there were safer and healthier alternatives to the garbage the drug companies were peddling and everyone was willingly taking. He wanted them to experience the benefits of treatment with botanicals. They're all natural, so there are no side effects. They work both inside and outside the body. And worst of all, compared to Big Pharma, they cost next to nothing. The big boys especially hated that last one.

"That's fantastic, Gabe! That's quite an inheritance he left you. Also, quite a heavy promise to keep," Ray noted.

"Well, that's what I wanted to talk to you about, Aloe Man." Gabe chuckled nervously, but Ray just raised his eyebrows as he often did when he heard something shocking.

"What would you think about using your garden here as a model for a new business, but blowing it up a hundred times larger. You have an opportunity to introduce the Aloe Age to the world and give it its rightful place in history. Hey, we had the Stone Age, the Ice Age, and the Bronze Age. Why not?"

Ray still wasn't sure where Gabe was going with this conversation and looked flummoxed. The euphoric effects of the spleef they shared were starting to kick in.

"So, no beating around the bush. Would you consider setting up and running the whole operation, because I know zilch about the growing end of the business, and you know more about it than anyone I know. I listened to you preaching about this wonder plant and I was amazed that you repeated everything my father used to say. Don't worry, I'll make sure you have everything you'll need to succeed. You'll never have to worry about money again, and you'll have a house to live in, and you'll have real purpose in your life. I swear to God, no jive, the sky's the limit! I will spare no expense to keep my father's promise."

"So, let me get this straight. Are you asking me if I'm willing to pack up and move to the high desert of southern Arizona, and just leave everything and everybody behind? I don't know, that would be awful tough. And what do I know about running a 400-acre aloe farm? I can barely manage what I have now. I can't begin to imagine the size and scale of that."

Gabe said he wouldn't have to give up his coach and abandon his garden. He suggested they leave the trailer and Ray's original Aloe Age garden as-is, and use it as their corporate headquarters and home base when they come back to visit. He also told him not to worry about handling all that he would be asked to do. First on the list was earning Ray's trust in him.

Ray told him it was a lot to absorb all at once, but appreciated considering him to take on such a colossal operation. There was more than a minute of dead silence while Gabe looked at Ray, who was staring pensively at the floor. He took a toke, held his breath, and let out a thick cloud of smoke. He looked up at Gabe through the haze.

"Whaddya ' say, Aloe Man? I'm telling you, it's the opportunity of a lifetime. You're gonna' hate yourself if you pass this up," Gabe teased with an anxious smile.

"Well, I hate to disappoint you man, but honestly, I can't give you an answer right now. I'm gonna' have to sleep on it."

CHAPTER TWENTY-THREE

"I wonder where the heck Gabe went?" Ray thought to himself as he pulled his gardening tools and equipment out of the shed in preparation for the day's work ahead of him.

He hadn't seen his new buddy and neighbor for more than a week, which he thought odd since Gabe seemed intent on getting an answer to his offer right away that night. Ray suspected Gabe would wait a few days for him to ruminate on it, and then check back to see where he was with his decision. He walked over to Gabe's coach to investigate his sudden disappearance. No one answered when Ray knocked on the door; no car, no note, no prior notice of his plans. It was like he simply vanished into thin air.

Walking back to his trailer, Ray spotted a bright yellow, familiar-looking VW bug heading his way. As it approached, Ray could make out through a filthy, bug-splattered windshield, the shadowy faces of Gabe sitting in the passenger seat, and his *compadre*, Fito, behind the wheel. He knew it had to be Fito because he remembered the vehicle from his earlier visit to Gabe's place.

From inside the bug, Gabe pointed out Ray and his garden as they drove by and parked. "That's the Aloe Man, Fito!" Then he shouted with a smile, "Yo, Ray! I'm back! Did you miss me?"

"Yeah, I actually did. You didn't tell me you were going away, so I got a little worried when I didn't see you for a few days. What if you died? What if you were toying with me with your offer and then disappeared? What if someone who knew your father's wealth kidnapped you and demanded a ransom? I know it sounds far out, but...."

Gabe was touched by Ray's concern and honesty. He admitted he should have notified Ray, but in his mind, he had been focused on surprising the Aloe Man with news that might influence his decision favorably.

"Sorry to cause you any worry, man," Gabe said sincerely. "While you've been thinking this over and trying to make a decision, me and Fito have been in Arizona getting the basic operation set up so that it's good to go for whomever takes it from there. We busted our tails and did a lot of heavy lifting out there. You'd be impressed."

It was about time for Ray's mid-morning coffee break, and also a perfect opportunity to talk about his plans and whether or not they included making this monumental move to Arizona.

"I made a decision based on my gut instincts, Gabe, and they came out of nowhere. I didn't know I had them in me. Now that I'm thinking more clearly, my brain helped me connect all the dots that I've seen in my head and in my dreams for some time now. It's all very weird, but at the same time, when I start piecing it together, it's starting to take shape and make some sense."

Gabe urged him to please continue and explain the dots he finally connected.

First, there was his time spent at Odyssey House learning the gardening basics but never expecting to take that knowledge and turn it into something worthwhile. Then he landed a landscaping job and tragically lost three fingers in a work accident, which put him in the hospital where he had that first dream. After that, it was the mystery delivery of plants that filled his garden and people took notice. He started schooling them on the wonders of aloe vera, then requests poured in to design aloe gardens and he started the Aloe Age business. And wonder of wonders, the icing on the cake was meeting Gabe. It was like God sent him a guardian angel from heaven."

He continued. "It feels like there's some strange, almost supernatural power that's pushing me. There have been too many signs to ignore. I never really paid much attention to them when they happened, and had no idea I'd ever find myself here and in this position. It must be the fickle finger of fate, pointing me in a different direction, down this new path, and taking me on some magic carpet ride to God knows where."

Ray revealed that in the past, he experienced what he believed could be an apparition by Jesus Christ, who told him he was the chosen one to introduce the new Aloe Age by bringing the gifts of nature and natural methods of healing to the masses instead of drugs. He said He was angry over the drug companies' evil greed and total disregard for the human souls He created that that have been destroyed. Above all, they broke His first commandment. They placed the false god of wealth and possession of material goods before Him.

As a disclaimer, he told Gabe he wasn't entirely sure, until now, it was in fact an apparition. For the longest time, he thought it also could possibly be an extreme acid flashback where he saw God, or an off-the-wall, psychedelic dream, weaving images of his time spent in the gardens at Odyssey House with the ethereal fantasy world of The Wizard of Oz's Emerald City.

"Then a few nights ago, I had another one of those trippy, super vivid dreams with the identical panoramic view as the first one, only it wasn't Jesus who appeared to me this time. Instead, it was a leather-faced Indian chief riding a white and brown Palomino. He looked directly at me and motioned with his hand to follow him to a valley far off in the distance that looked kinda' like the way I always pictured the Garden of Eden would look. It was like he was showing me this is the pathway to finding nirvana."

Despite feeling a tinge of separation anxiety, Ray agreed to Gabe's gracious offer and they immediately sealed the deal with a handshake and a bear hug. In celebration, they passed a joint and talked well into the night about logistics and a timetable. There would be a lot to do in preparation for the move and little time to waste. Besides the wisps of smoke and aroma of pot coming from the coach, there was a palpable feeling of anticipation and wonderment hanging in the night air.

CHAPTER TWENTY-FOUR

D-Day finally arrived; today was the day of departure for Ray and Gabe. There would be no turning back now. It was officially go-time.

They loaded the stake-bed with most of their worldly possessions and every tool and piece of equipment Ray owned. They double-checked that the guitar and saxophone were aboard. They knew they would occasionally need their music to soothe the savage beast that awaited them.

Ray took a moment to soak in the magnitude of the life-changing decision he was making. Living a few hundred steps from the Pacific Ocean, he was trading a near idyllic existence on the west coast of California for sweltering heat and a barren wasteland that was excruciating and unforgiving to the unprepared. He would no longer have Bonnie Lee nearby to act as his personal safety net if and when he stumbled and fell, or crashed and burned. But deep down in his soul, he knew he could assuredly count on Gabe to have his six when he needed it. Ray had grown to trust him implicitly in the relatively short time they'd known one another.

For some strange reason, Ray hadn't given much thought to driving 12 hours in a loaded down truck over mountains and into the desert, but it was finally dawning on him now. He dreaded driving on the busy freeways because of the noise and the speed of passing vehicles, and heavy traffic, and he avoided them whenever he could. This would be his first road trip in a while, and he was beginning to feel a few butterflies fluttering in his gut. The best way to quiet them and ease his mind would be to get on the road.

The truck was all gassed up and declared road ready directly from the mouth of Ray's mechanic, who went over it with a fine-toothed comb the day before, looking for anything sketchy. Ray asked him to make sure the fluids, hoses, and tires were in ship shape because this trip would put the truck to a test. They had plenty of water, a bag full of fruit, a thermos of coffee, and some beef jerky.

Ray was gripping as soon as he merged the Toyota into heavy, slow-moving midday traffic on I-5 south along the coast. He was hyper-focused, leaning forward in the driver's seat, white knuckling the wheel, with his eyeballs bugging out watching the vehicle in front of him. Gabe didn't dare interfere with his driving or distract him with idle conversation, so there was a cone of silence while Ray navigated through four lanes of bumper-to-bumper traffic. They were hoping they'd catch one of those lucky breaks that occur at random times during the day when traffic is suddenly and inexplicably light for 10 or 15 minutes, but it wasn't in the cards that day. Departing at a fortuitous hour determined whether or not they'd make good time. This adventure could be either a dream or a nightmare, and totally unpredictable. It wasn't off to a rousing start.

Ray relaxed a tad once they cleared the downtown congestion and escaped from the endless backups that come with millions of people with cars living in paradise. Now, here he was, on his way to living a dream he promised to live, although it was with a measure of uncertainty as to exactly how it all becomes a reality. It would be a miracle if it actually happened, but he believed in miracles. He leaned back in his seat, loosened his grip on the steering wheel, and even managed to finally open his mouth and speak.

"Holy Moley, sure glad we're out of that mess. That was intense as hell, man!"

Gabe agreed and complimented Ray on his stellar driving. Sounding a note of optimism, he assured Ray it would be smooth sailing from there, assuming they didn't experience any mechanical problems or backups. The four-cylinder stake bed struggled mightily climbing those formidable mountains, and hauling a full load didn't help. With the added strain placed on the truck and the temperature now rising to the mid-90s, Ray said a quick prayer to the patron saint of mechanics to bless the recent inspection and tune-up. This was no place to break down. There was nothing but land and sky in every direction as far as the eye could see; help would be hours away if at all. Fortunately, they made plans and were prepared for such an emergency should one befall them, which is about all anyone can do when driving through the desert, and agreed it would be best if they just put it in God's hands to work out.

Gabe suggested they exit the interstate and drive the less-traveled back roads through some of the tiny villages and hamlets in the county's backcountry. It would make a far more relaxed and leisurely ride and they'd get to see sights they normally wouldn't if they stayed on the interstate. They stopped in the village of Julian, locally famous for their apples and enormous, heavyweight apple pies. The smell of the pies baking is pumped out through strategically-placed exhaust fans, where it lingers in the air long enough to lure customers in.

Gabe and Ray fell under the spell of the smell. They couldn't resist the urge to purchase one, knowing a slice of apple pie would be a wise choice for solving a case of the munchies. They drove through aptly named Idyllwild, a tiny, touristy outpost where the friendly townies informed them that the dog they were so cheerfully petting was in fact Idyllwild's mayor. Yes indeed, the citizenry actually elected a popular golden retriever named Bud to take care of the town's business. And he did it his own way.

Just about every day, without fail, Mayor Bud freely roamed off-leash and, unaccompanied through the pedestrian-only town, casually dropped in on merchants who happily put out bowls of water or offered him a treat. He drew attention wherever he wandered, welcoming visitors, tongue hanging out, tail wagging, drooling but wearing a smile and a red bandana around his neck, all the while serving as Idyllwild's goodwill ambassador of sorts. He was a bona fide attraction, which tended to draw visitors, who in turn spend money and ring cash registers. Bud's always pleasant disposition put smiles on people's faces, and when people are happy and smiling, life in general seems better.

Onward they cruised, up and over the Cuyamaca Mountains and through the surrounding sacred Native American tribal land once inhabited by the Kumeyaay band. Ray's eyes darted left and right as he drove, oddly admiring the craggy, sharply-angled rock faces silhouetted against mostly barren, wide open spaces clear to the horizon line, where land meets sky.

Gabe peered over at Ray with squinty eyes and asked him to confirm that he saw Ray's face light up, and he seemed more relaxed and comfortable behind the wheel.

"Excellent idea, brother," Ray replied, "Let's light up. Here ya' go." He handed Gabe a fatty he pulled out of a Marlboro box and pushed in the dashboard lighter. "No worries. It's cool out here. Nobody's gonna' hassle us," he assured him, sensing some hesitancy. When the lighter popped out, Ray grabbed it and held it for Gabe to light. He took a few puffs and passed it to Ray, covering his mouth with his hand trying to stifle the smoke-induced explosion taking place in his lungs.

Ray laughed and acknowledged the herb's high potency, and then revealed the source: his sister, Bonnie Lee. Knowing his fondness for herb, she asked her U.S. Marine Corps MP husband if he might have the ability to make an ounce of confiscated contraband disappear. She wanted to give Ray a going away present he would appreciate, and fondly remember them by.

"My old musician friend Ricardo and I went camping up here a few times," Ray began. "He's a drummer, and we met through another musician friend, and hit it off immediately, and then worked together for years playing in bands and writing and recording original music. Every single night we'd be in his home studio, first getting Irie and amped up on coffee, and then collaborating and creating our own style of music. Our name was Golden Rule because we both believed in that concept as a guide for living your life. We felt it was an important message to send to people through music. Yeah, Ricardo was an awesome partner; could be a jackass at times, but what partner isn't guilty of that?"

Ray went on telling Gabe how much Ricardo loved nature and being out in it whenever he could, and he often dragged him along for company. While on a road trip camped in a redwood forest, he and Ricardo took a guitar and bongos, and a handful of psychedelic mushrooms, and hiked from their campsite deep into the woods by the light of a full moon. They sat on the ground and started an improvised jam that went on for nearly an hour. To an outsider listening in, their playing may have been all over the map musically, but it hit the sweet spot on some spiritual level that left an indelible mark on their minds and souls. It was an extraordinary musical experience they cherished and would stay with them for a lifetime.

Gabe asked what happened to Ricardo?

Ray said he moved back east where he was originally from, coincidentally not all that far from the town where Ray grew up. Ricardo lost his father, brother and mother in one year, and decided he wanted to be closer to his remaining family. It had been quite a few years since he saw him last.

"I miss that dude," he said fondly. "We were like brothers, and spent an awful lot of time together. He had solid meter and we could always count on him to play in the pocket. I sure was sad to see him go, but he did what he felt he had to do."

With a mellow buzz on, they faced the daunting Banning Grade, a serpentine two-lane stretch of asphalt that greatly tested Ray's concentration and mettle as a novice road tripper. This route wasn't for the faint of heart; a relentless series of hairpin turns and super-tight S-curves, one after another, and no guard rails on either side of the road. Ray didn't care to look out his window at the unimaginable fate that awaited them should he lose control and plunge over the edge. He was told many have over the years.

Toward the bottom of the grade, the narrow road eventually leveled out straight into an appealing assortment of bucolic farms and ranch land. They entered sparsely populated Ramona, which had a general store, a gas station, a locally famous bakery, a Catholic church, and a tavern. Most everybody who lived in Ramona either owned massive farms that bred and trained thoroughbred horses, or they raised beef cattle that grazed on miles and miles of open range grasslands.

From there, they caught County Road S-4, another steep, corkscrew of a grade with needle-sharp curves and harrowing, pretzel-twisting turns. Ray had his eyes glued to the road, but caught a slight distraction peripherally as he navigated the two-lane roadway carved through the mountain. He dared not let his eyes stray even for an instant. That's all it would take for him to make the gravest of errors. On the final turn, they were rewarded with a splendiferous panorama that turned out to be the source of his earlier distraction.

A thick, undulating carpet of pink sand verbena stretched out in every direction. It gradually blended into a giant palette of colorful chuparosa, towering ocotillos, stout barrel cactus and agave, dune evening primrose, and the ghastly looking ghost flower. As good fortune would have it, their timing couldn't have been better if they tried. A desert in full bloom spread out gloriously before them like a personal welcome mat, and what a breathtaking sight it was. Ray had no words that could fully describe to others this majestic vision of loveliness, or to fully express the grandiosity of God's genius and greatness. He just kept shaking his head, alternately in disbelief and then in mind-blowing amazement at the Almighty's incredible handiwork.

"I heard people talking about this wonder of nature, but I wrote it off as exaggeration. Man, was I wrong. I had no idea it was this big and there was this much color to see," Ray admitted.

Gabe briefly explained that when winter's rains are heavy and drenching enough, they soak deep into the ground and germinate the seed pods that laid dormant several inches below the surface, sometimes for several years. What results is a rare spectacle of nature that arrives all dressed up for dinner.

Ray silently panned the desolate landscape and couldn't stop praising the raw beauty and elegance he found everywhere he turned. The 360 degree view resembled scenes out of the cowboys and Indians movies or shoot-em-up western shows he watched on TV as a kid. Absorbing the immensity of it, as incomprehensible as that was, also revealed to Ray just how comparatively minuscule and insignificant he was. The moment had the odd effect of literally putting him in his rightful place in the universe where he was suddenly made aware he was no more than a drop in the ocean or a grain of sand in the desert.

Right outside of the city of Calexico near the California-Arizona border, they ran into warnings of high winds that soon after kicked up a blinding dust storm that forced them to pull into a rest area and hunker down until it passed. With the windows rolled up tight to keep the dust out, they sat in the sweltering truck with no air conditioning and gnawed on ostrich jerky, topped off with a hunk of the apple pie they scored in Julian. Gabe looked out and saw the winds had died down and visibility improved enough to hit the road again.

A group of about 20 Mexican laborers mustered nearby noticed the maroon stake bed truck when the dust cleared, and they instantly swarmed, hoping for a chance to get hired for the day. The men surrounded it and blocked them from moving, then started banging on the windows and begging, *"por favor, senor!"* Ray and Gabe tried desperately to explain they were moving to Arizona, not hiring. Ray knew a little bit of Spanish from working with Earl and Drew and blurted out, *"No trabajo aquí! Vamos!"* while vigorously shaking his head and waving his hands accentuating the word "no."

Gabe asked for a translation. "I told them we don't have any work and to split," Ray replied. "By the dirty looks they gave me when they were walking away, they seemed none too pleased, so I guess they understood."

Before they got rolling again, Gabe told Ray to wait a minute while he grabbed two sodas from an ice chest in the bed. It seemed like he was taking forever, but when he finally returned, he looked like he just saw a ghost. Ray was about to ask what happened when Gabe cut him off and motioned him to the back of the truck. There, he pointed to a big empty space where the guitar and sax once were.

CHAPTER TWENTY-FIVE

Mildly in the state of shock over having just become a victim of a robbery, never mind getting played by a pack of punk-ass *cucarachas*, Ray looked down and shook his head dejectedly. He leaned against the truck and crossed his arms, quietly seething inside. Then he looked skyward toward the heavens, as if to shout out to God and ask, "Why is this happening?"

Gabe placed a comforting hand on Ray's shoulder and tried to assure him the instruments would be replaced with brand new ones and they'd eventually grow to appreciate those as much as their old ones.

"I know, you can always buy another brand new one, but that there guitar can't ever be replaced," Ray explained with a tone of deep regret in his voice.

"My sister bought it and gave it to me right before I left. It's a brand spanking new Guild six-string that I was planning on surprising you with when we got to wherever we're going. Never even got to play it once."

Gabe understood Ray's anger and disappointment, and agreed a new instrument could never take the place of one with that amount of sentimental value. As a way to offer some consolation, he confessed to Ray his horn had significant sentimental value as well.

"My daddy gave me that horn, which his daddy passed down to him," Gabe said, pointing out the family's proud line of ownership for three generations that made his loss especially painful.

"God, I'm sorry, Gabe. That's tragic, man. You'll never get that sound back," Ray said, shaking his head in disgust. "C'mon, let's get outta' here."

They crossed the state line into Arizona and proceeded south and east on a lonely state road that ran parallel to the Mexico border. There was still a couple hundred miles to cover before they reached their final destination, and the sun was just beginning its lazy descent, but they had a few hours of daylight driving left.

They hadn't seen any traffic in either direction for nearly 50 miles, which suited Ray just fine. He was still fired up over the grand larceny that was just perpetrated on them, but he refused to let that become a dark cloud overshadowing the courageous endeavor he was embarking on. He and Gabe chalked it up to God's sometimes inexplicable will, and the Lord working in the most mysterious of ways. They thought perhaps a quick attitude adjustment would help lift their spirits.

Ray instinctively checked his rear view mirror, quickly removed his sunglasses, and checked the mirror again. He said he thought he saw a flash but it must have been sunlight reflecting on a piece of glass or chrome. A minute later, he saw it again, and then again, and it got closer, and closer, until he finally recognized the distant flashes in his rear view mirror were emergency lights. They belonged to the United States Border Patrol unit that was fast approaching the Toyota. Ray figured they were in hot pursuit of illegals so he pulled off to the shoulder as legally required to give them the right of way. Instead, Border Patrol followed them to the shoulder and two strapping young officers emerged from the unit and walked up on each side of the truck. Ray and Gabe turned and looked at each other at the exact same time, wordlessly wondering the exact same thought: where'd we hide the pot? They knew it was too late to start acting herky-jerky and giving these good 'ol boys cause to search for any contraband. They were forced to sit still and act nonchalantly while their stomachs were getting tied into knots.

U.S. Border Patrol Officer Alejandro Guzman asked Ray for his license and registration, which he had at the ready and courteously handed over. He looked it over and walked back to the unit chatting with his partner. Ray and Gabe were sweating bullets from the roasting heat outside, and from the "heat" of the law that was sitting in the car right behind them. Only God knew the fate awaited them. A flood of nightmare scenarios rushed through their minds, and momentarily distracted them from the officers approaching the vehicle.

"We were wondering if you guys have anything missing out of your truck... like these?," Officer Guzman asked with a devious smile as he held up the pilfered guitar and saxophone. It took a few seconds for the reality of the outlandish situation to finally sink in, and when it did, they tried to speak but couldn't produce the words. They were frozen with emotion. Ray was so emotional and overcome with gratitude that he started bawling; not only at getting the instruments back, but the herculean efforts the Border Patrol made to see they were returned to their rightful owners. Ray and Gabe never in their wildest dreams imagined they would see that new guitar and vintage sax again, and were effusively appreciative. Ray was dying to know how they were able to recover the stolen goods, and so quickly.

Officer Guzman explained that he and his partner had the muster group under ground and aerial surveillance. After spotting them swarming the truck and grabbing the instruments, they moved in, and when the group saw it was Border Patrol, they all scattered and dropped the loot. Everyone got away, but the officers grabbed the two cases. They got the truck's location from the aerial surveillance team and hot tailed it out there to hand-deliver a miraculous conclusion to what began as a tragically ugly story of disrespect, deception, thievery, and ill-will toward one's fellow man.

Ray wondered out loud whether someone was watching over them, like a guardian angel, or if they were simply the benefactors of plain dumb luck. Or maybe it was a little of both, but nonetheless, Ray finally witnessed a case of Murphy's Law in reverse. They couldn't give the officers a cash gratuity as a token of their appreciation and for their service far, far, far beyond the call of duty. Instead, they offered them two slices of apple pie and a few pieces of buffalo jerky, which the officers graciously accepted and admitted was a first for them.

After shaking their hands and promising the men a reward sometime in the not-to-distant future for doing their good deed for the day, Ray and Gabe were cruising again, mesmerized by the endless heat waves radiating off the blistering hot pavement. It wasn't too long before the sun finished working its day shift and was officially off-duty. The darkening shadows of dusk cast a veil of heaviness on Ray's eyelids and it was apparent they weren't going to safely complete the journey in one day as they had hoped. Unexpected and unavoidable delays forced them to seek shelter for the night at a roadside motel outside of Nogales, where they showered, grabbed a few hours of shut eye, and then set out refreshed in the morning to complete the final stretch. Besides ensuring their safety, it was important to Gabe that Aloe Man get his first glimpse of Aloe Age

City in broad daylight and in its full glory, and not under the cover of darkness. That wouldn't do it justice.

CHAPTER TWENTY-SIX

Those pesky butterflies were all aflutter in Ray's gut the moment he opened his eyes and realized where he was. He was only a couple of hours away from the great project unveiling, and his imagination was running wild with nervous excitement about his future, and what it might look like in six months, or a year or two or five. Where will he be physically, mentally, emotionally, spiritually, even musically? Will the experience be a positive or negative one, and good for the soul or bad?

It was going to take time and patience to find the answers to those questions, and the biggest one would be whether he had the wherewithal to go the full distance – very much unknown to him at that moment in time – and have the moxie to tough it out when the road got extra rocky. Gabe never once promised it was going to be a cake walk. He did say don't sweat the details, but that didn't mean this undertaking would be a tiptoe through the tulips.

Rolling along the southern Arizona border and venturing into the lunar landscape that defined rural Cochise County, they turned northward and made their way to Tombstone, then through the Dragoon Mountains, and down into tiny Dos Cabezas. No more than a mere speck on the Rand-McNally Road Atlas map of Arizona, the town bordered a drab and desolate Cochise Indian reservation where the only business was a single-pump gas station that stocked a few groceries but mainly was the reservation's sole source of beer and cigarettes. Interestingly, sales of Carbona Rug Cleaner were steadily through the roof and it wasn't because everyone on the reservation loved to clean their carpets so often.

Sadly, a lot of them were rabid huffers. Containing a laundry list of toxic and poisonous chemicals, rug cleaner was cheap, fast-acting, easy to obtain, and entirely legal. The devastatingly sad result was pitiful gangs of stuporous, brain-damaged vagrants who spent their entire day, every day, inhaling vapors that completely destroy their minds and bodies. They couldn't do a day's work even if they wanted to because they could barely function. They received a monthly stipend from the gubmint simply for their birthright as a Native American residing on an Indian reservation, and they used a hefty portion of it on alcohol, tobacco, and untold cans full of dangerous chemicals that have no mercy on the body and take no prisoners.

Ray noticed the gateway welcome sign and after making a quick translation in his head, he looked askance at Gabe.

"You know what that means?" he asked. Gabe quickly replied, "Yeah, two heads. Why?"

"I'm just trying to figure out if there's some kind of deeper meaning going on here, like the two heads represent me and you, or us and God, or it just so happened that the land your father purchased falls within the legal boundaries of the town of Dos Cabezas. You gotta' admit, Gabe, the name does seem to have some cosmic possibilities, right?"

Gabe chuckled, and then explained that his father did take into account the relevance of the town's name when he bought the land.

"Ever since I was a little kid, he always told me that two heads were better than one, so yeah, that was part of it," Gabe said. "I think he wanted me to be a part of this, you know, the second head, but he never actually said so. Maybe he wanted to see if I'd ask to join him. But look, here I am doing exactly what I believe he wanted me to do. And if not for you Aloe Man, I don't think I would have fulfilled a dream he had for me. So, I have you to thank for that. Without even knowing, you did me a huge favor by accepting my offer."

A half-mile beyond a line of adobes and ceremonial teepees that lined the reservation's border, Ray began to see the faint outlines of some unusual looking figures breaking the distant skyline. He quickly determined they definitely were not of the saguaro cactus and sagebrush variety he'd seen for the last hundred or so miles.

"Jesus, are those cranes I'm looking at?" he asked Gabe incredulously. He smiled back at Ray and said, "Ah! I love the sight of cranes in the air! That's the sign of progress right there, brother. That's thinking big. They do the heavy lifting that makes possible what ordinarily would be considered impossible."

They drove closer and the picture became larger and in sharper focus, and it was almost too much for Ray to absorb all at once. He was slack jawed at the first sight of it, and temporarily took his eyes off the winding road. Next thing he knew the truck drifted over a double yellow line into the oncoming lane and he had to quickly correct to avoid a motorcyclist that was headed right for them and flashing his headlight. After regaining his composure, and catching his breath, Gabe calmly but firmly pointed out that it would be a crying shame to fumble the ball at the goal line by having a fatal wreck. They'd come too far and been through too much hell. Ray certainly couldn't argue with that and appreciated the wisdom of Gabe's football analogy.

Ray imagined a chorus of trumpets blaring out a warm welcome to him and Gabe when they pulled the exhausted stake bed into the driveway of their new compound, which was under construction everywhere they turned. Work crews were building at a breakneck pace; a sprawling ranch-style home, a humongous greenhouse the size of a football field, a few pole barns, production and storage facilities, a spa that featured natural hot springs and sulphur springs, surrounded by rustic cabins, juice bars and a farm-to-table restaurant. Encircling it all were the biggest, healthiest, juiciest, prize-winning aloe vera barbadensis plants he'd ever seen, and there were literally thousands of them. The sheer number that were planted was even more astounding than their perfect size, shape, and color.

Then, Ray's eyes were drawn to those cranes, their arms outstretched and reaching for the sky.

"Let's walk over there so I can show you what's going on," Gabe said. "Pretty cool stuff that I remembered from some of our wilder conversations about your vision of the ideal sustainable garden."

"Well, there it is, Aloe Man," Gabe said, pointing to a crane hoisting a massive slab of copper. "There's the first piece of your monument to sustainability using nature's way of healing and health. This will be Aloe Man's modern-day take on the Fountain of Youth."

"Hey, we could name the company Nature's Way. But we'd have to add a Z or something because there's a song by Spirit with that title."

True to form as a visionary and big idea man, Gabe wanted to build a monument – a 150-foot tall replica of an aloe vera barbadensis

– that would exceed the dimensions of the 1964 World's Fair's famous Unisphere and displace it in the Guiness Book of Records as the world's largest outdoor metal sculpture. He wanted it sculpted out of copper so that when it oxidized, the patina would closely resemble the plant's exquisite greenish-blue hues. It was also meant to be a monument to his father and his dream.

Ray was absolutely giddy trying to conjure up an image of a 150-foot tall aloe vera plant. As a devotee and collector of art and sculpture, Gabe's father had a number of sculpted pieces he kept in storage, and Gabe planned to set them free and display them in a sprawling sculpture park he designed as part of the compound. One piece that his dad commissioned and was particularly proud to own was a giant bronze sundial, which he felt should stand as a reminder to use our time here wisely. It was to serve as a symbol of returning to basics, using the shadows cast by the sun to tell roughly the time of day. Gabe thought it could be a fascinating attraction and a subtle way to deliver his father's powerful messages: time doesn't stand still, and to make the most of it. That included getting back to making Mother Earth the wellspring of health and wellness.

Gabe suggested they unload the Toyota and get settled in their temporary home while the permanent one was being built. Ray didn't notice it at first coming up the driveway, but when he passed the new construction, he got a big surprise. For the next few months, they'd be living in a trailer in the middle of no-man's land that was as close to hell on earth as it possibly gets. Ray reminded himself that he was a heat freak because he was about to get a heavy dose and steady diet of it.

This wasn't just any old coach plopped down willy-nilly somewhere in hell's half acre. Ray looked around and noticed that the place looked oddly familiar. It was deja vu all over again.

"Hey, this looks like my place back home!" Ray exclaimed as the light bulb in his head lit up.

"Exactly!" Gabe answered. "I wanted to make sure you felt right at home, so I recreated it here so it'd look familiar. How do you like it?"

Ray was amazed at the details and nuances Gabe skillfully replicated, right down to the layout of the gardens where he grew his own fruit, herbs, and vegetables adjacent to the aloes. With no shortage of sunshine and a paucity of rain, even the hardiest of drought-resistant succulents get thirsty and need an occasional drink of water. Gabe was already making plans to install an elaborate irrigation and pump system powered by an enormous wind and solar farm. He again credited his father Raymond, for seeing more environmentally friendly energy out on the horizon and wanting to bring it closer to home. It was part of his focus on sustainability that ultimately extends the life of the planet we inhabit.

They sat at the tiny kitchen table where Gabe had the plans spread out. Ray noticed another stack of plans off to the side and asked what they were for.

"Wait 'til you see these plans my dad drew up, Ray. It's gonna' blow your mind. If we pull this off, this is gonna' be a mecca of the west, where people from all over the world can gather to rejuvenate and re-energize their spiritual and physical health and well-being and have a space to reflect on applying it to their everyday lives."

Gabe explained that they were essentially building an entirely new Dos Cabezas and Cochise Nation. The town would graduate to cityhood and with Mr. Gabe's billions, build a new school, an interdenominational place of worship, a hospital, bank, supermarket, drug store/commercial strip mall for small businesses, a movie theater/bowling alley, and a department store, along with an expanded power grid and infrastructure improvements. All right next door to the reservation and within walking distance.

Besides having access to these brand new basic amenities, the true beauty of the plan was that the tribal members living in squalor and near poverty on the reservation, with little to no education, no job skills, and ultimately a bleak future, would reap a great many benefits and rewards from all the development. From his business travel, Raymond's eyes had been opened to the struggles Native Americans face every day, and he wisely included solutions to address some of those challenges in the detailed plans he left his son. Otherwise, they would remain stuck in the quagmire that their collective lives had become and with no hope to escape. If not for celebrating their heritage and long-held traditions, they would have practically nothing to live for. His intention was to brighten their outlook by providing them with basic tools they needed to begin building new and improved lives.

The plans called for the tribe to receive a generous portion of the profits from all commercial ventures, which would then be distributed in the form of monthly dividends to the tribal members. The businesses would generate steady employment and guaranteed income for anyone who wanted to work, and there would be no outside competition from retail and fast-food chains or big box stores. Land developers were prohibited from purchasing reservation land and building new homes, preventing a flood of new residents. It was important to preserve the delicate balance between the fragile environment and the livelihoods of those already living there.

CHAPTER TWENTY-SEVEN

"How the hell were you able to get all of this stuff going in the time you were gone? It seems impossible," Ray asked of Gabe. "It's unreal. It's...

"...a miracle, I know," Gabe said, completing his sentence. "My father had all of this lined up and he was ready to pull the trigger. And when you know very powerful and influential people in high places, and with enough money, of course, well, you can see that anything's possible. But hey, this is only the beginning. We've got a ton of hard work ahead of us. Dad did a fantastic job of setting the table, and now we have to get busy in the kitchen to prepare and serve up the dish."

"That's deep, Gabe. A really brilliant way to look at it." Ray paused for a few seconds, then added jokingly, "The kitchen and meal analogy suddenly made me hungry, though. Whaddya' say we womp up some hot dogs and beans?"

Gabe was on board, and as they got up from the table, Ray heard a noise outside that he recognized immediately from his landscaping days. It was the distinctive "Call to the Post" that's played before the start of every horse race. It blasted out of the roof-mounted horn of a roach coach, which preceded its arrival on a job site. Right on cue, the workers immediately stopped whatever they were doing and queued up at the window.

"You thinking what I'm thinking," Ray asked Gabe.

"Forget the hot dogs. Let's get in line," Gabe replied.

The food truck was owned by a hardworking husband and wife from Mexico, who traveled to Dos Cabezas from the small town of Wilcox, about 25 miles to the north. The volume of business they were doing made the trip worth their while. Gabe and Ray brought up the back of the line and mingled with the tradesmen – heavy equipment operators, carpenters, masons, roofers, electricians, plumbers, painters – and when it was their turn, they ordered a couple of carne asada burritos with rice and beans.

Back at the coach, Ray pulled two cold Tecates out of an ice chest, handed one to Gabe. They tapped the longneck bottles together and took a big, long swig. There was no need to speak any words. The ching-ching of the bottles said it all and seemed to resonate throughout the trailer. It was the final commitment that symbolically sealed their deal and confirmed their commitment to support both the project and each other. That sound toasted the good fortune that awaited them, assuming they followed the plan and took all the steps to get it right.

The burritos and frosty cold beers hit the spot, and afterward, they broke out the new Guild guitar and the sax, rolled up a joint of Bonnie Lee's high-test herb, and kicked back just like they did when they were back home jamming in Ray's coach. Perhaps he was just a tad too stoned, but Ray admitted he actually thought he was there for a moment. He had a laugh at himself, which meant he was clearly comfortable and showing no signs of separation anxiety. Gabe was worried about Ray's adjustment to a new life in strange and unfamiliar surroundings, but he put those fears to rest when he saw how relaxed Ray appeared. On the other hand, a couple of Tecates and sharing a joint of Maui Wowie might have had something to do with his mood. Gabe thought that once the haze of intoxication lifted, he'd get a more accurate read on Ray's real state of mind.

"Pop! Pssshhtt!" "Pop! Pssshhtt!" "Pop! Pssshhtt!" "Pop! Pssshhtt!"

They instantly put down their instruments and bolted to the closest window to discover the source of the popping and hissing. When they looked out, all they saw were red taillights with the distinctive look of a mid-1960s Ford Mustang speeding away. Ray found a flashlight, went outside, and walked over to his truck. Just as he suspected: all four tires punctured and slashed. When he walked around and looked closer, he saw that the truck's gas cap was lying on the ground next to an empty sack of sugar.

"Appears as if there are some people who don't like us and 'aint happy that we're here," Ray muttered, stating the obvious. "So in just one day we have enemies and no mode of transportation."

Gabe responded with his typical glass half-full optimism to counter Ray's glass half-empty pessimism.

"Fear not, Aloe Man! I arranged to have a bunch of new farm equipment delivered and will just ask them to throw in a new truck. No worries, we'll order new tires and get a mechanic out here and see if we can get this beast to run again. Might have to put in a new engine, who knows. Chin up! Have faith! It's not the end of the world, my friend."

Just more of the same old crap to deal with, Ray complained. In this case, Gabe suspected the vandalism was committed by a gang of tweakers who lived on the reservation. They supplied the addicts who could afford the "good stuff" and didn't have to resort to huffing rug cleaner to get their fix. They cooked the methamphetamine in a bathtub by mixing highly flammable and hazardous chemicals with the epinephrine found in cold capsules and prayed the volatile concoction wouldn't explode and burn down the house or kill the people inside.

As the only player in the game, the dealers had a virtual monopoly on business and a loyal customer base on the reservation and in the surrounding towns, and they received protection from the tribal police and local law enforcement, many of whom were meth addicts themselves. They knew that nobody would be held accountable for the act of vandalism and the property damage, so it was futile to report it to the police. Gabe and Ray felt it would only make matters worse and certainly wouldn't endear them further to their new neighbors.

There's never an excuse for criminal and bad behavior, however, the drug world was the only way these misfits knew how to make money and survive. With opportunities so limited, so are the choices they have. It's often generational and difficult to break the chain when a kid's drug-addled parents are grooming him or her to make the drug trade their lives. For most of them, they have to choose one side or the other: either make or sell drugs, or become a lifetime user and loser. Some choice.

CHAPTER TWENTY-EIGHT

Ray wasn't about to settle for anything less than an exact replica of the burgundy-colored, low-mileage, 1979 Toyota stake bed truck that carried them and their load to this strange land. He was eccentric, one might even say pig-headed, that way. He was comfortable driving that particular make and model, so the replacement had to match. The specified color was a tribute to, and a sentimental reminder of, the original. Gabe made an attempt to persuade him to go with an aloe-like green, which his supplier could have there in a day or two, but Ray wouldn't budge on burgundy. It took his brand loyalty to an incredibly new, and frustrating, level.

That stubbornness delayed the new truck's delivery; what was expected to take a couple of days turned into more than a week while a mad search was on for a vehicle that precisely met Ray's annoying specifications. The result was no transportation to run errands or work on the aloe farms and gardens. While Gabe sympathized with his attachment to the truck, he firmly conveyed the message that the wheels of this operation had to keep turning, literally and figuratively, and his pettiness was taking all of the wind out of their sails.

Basic food and household supplies were getting low, so they decided to make an early morning run to the reservation store and pick up a few items to hold them over until they were mobile once again. They walked a mile or so on lonely County Road 186 just as the day was beginning to heat up. When they arrived, they were met with nasty looks and undercurrents of incoherent mumbling and grumbling. These poor souls weren't easy on the eyes. Rode hard and put away wet, as horse people say. They had scabs and open sores all over their pasty white faces. The occasional laugh or smile revealed blackened rotted teeth. They looked dirty, appeared angry, and acted downright hostile.

Gabe and Ray ignored the dagger-like stares and walked past them into the smelly, dimly-lit, Quonset hut structure. It was their first time inside the place and when they saw it, they were shocked at the utter disarray and mostly empty shelves. They were able to scare up a box of Saltine crackers, peanut butter and strawberry jelly, and a couple of overripe avocados that would have to do. Ray grabbed a six-pack of beer, a bag of *chicharrones*, and a couple of Hershey bars. Checking out at the counter, he tried to make small talk with the owner but got nothing in return and not even the barest hint of a smile or appreciation for their patronage, such that it was. He asked for a bag of ice, a few lighters, and rolling papers.

"Read the sign," came the reply from behind the cash register, along with a finger pointing to the wall behind him. It was the standard, "We reserve the right to refuse service to anyone for any reason."

"So then, is the reason for your refusal to sell us certain goods based on the fact that you automatically hate us without even knowing who we are or what we're doing here? Because we're considered outsiders? Not one of you?"

"Here's your change, now beat it and don't come back. I don't want your business. And we don't need the business you're bringing here."

"Pity," Gabe retorted, "because it's going to put this armpit of a town on the map, and change it in a good way. And hey, just so you know, we're not going anywhere, no matter how much you try to frighten us into leaving. We're dug in deep; we're here to stay, come hell or high water. Nobody's trying to do you any harm, or mess with the pathetic lives you live. So I suggest you all get used to us being here."

Gabe was fired up and tossed the groceries in his backpack, turned to Ray and said with fervor, "We gotta' get outta' this place, Aloe Man! There's way too much bad mojo. Feels like the devil lives here."

The Aloe Man moniker didn't escape the bitter ears of the bigoted loser at the counter. What is this Aloe Man nonsense? Does this wingnut granola muncher, flower power freak from California really think he's some kind of superhero, like the Elastic Man or the Invisible Man? Does he wear a cape and a giant A painted on his chest?

The disgruntled pair exited past the tweakers, who were laughing and sniggering at the owner shutting down their request for the extra items. Ray and Gabe refused to respond to the chatter and kept their gaze fixed on the ground to avoid any eye contact that could lead to a confrontation, physical or otherwise. As soon as they reached the highway, their nasal passages were assaulted by the acrid smell of a brush fire or wood burning. They looked up and saw columns of thick, black smoke billowing from the direction of Aloe Age Farm. Alarm bells went off in their minds simultaneously and they both immediately broke into a full-on sprint back to the compound to investigate and prayed that the blaze was burning anywhere but there. Another loss and disruption would just about break them and send a final message, in case they missed the previous ones, that the whole experiment was never meant to be. There was positively no way the planets were in alignment judging by all that went wrong so far.

They might have thrown in the towel right then and there if not for the scene that unfolded as they ran up the driveway and watched in horror as flames shot through the roof and engulfed most of their temporary shelter. All of the workers on the job site had formed a bucket brigade stretching from an irrigation pond to the front door of the trailer in a last-ditch attempt to salvage whatever hadn't yet burned. In the end, their efforts were no match for the blaze, and they were forced to stand down and watch it burn.

A day laborer from the reservation called Eagle Eye whom Ray befriended a few days earlier, approached him and offered an eyewitness account. A small car drove up slowly, turned around, and then one of the passengers threw a flaming object, most likely a Molotov cocktail, through a window of the trailer and then hot-tailed it out of there. He said the place went up like a box of wooden matches.

Ray asked if he got a look at the vehicle and the man replied he was fairly certain it was a Ford Mustang because he caught a glimpse of the model's telltale rear lights. That meant the same crew that damaged the truck to render them immobile now upped their game to arson as a way to terrorize them into saying "uncle" and packing it in. The question they repeatedly asked themselves but didn't dare yet verbalize, was "who needs the constant aggravation, the hatred of us, the constant threats and ill will?

The next day, once the smoke cleared and the smoldering ruins were finally extinguished, Gabe and Ray sifted through the remnants in search of any evidence and personal belongings that remained. They didn't have much to begin with, but what they brought with them were the bare essentials: some food, work clothes, camp cots and sleeping bags, a lantern, and of course, their treasured instruments. Now those basic items were gone in the time it took to walk to the store and back, and there was nothing left of any value from their material world.

A portion of the sheet metal roof fell into the galley area since there was no longer a structure supporting it, and it was still in one piece. Gabe and Ray lifted it up to check what was underneath and, Eureka! The instruments were there, tucked away safely and undamaged in their hard cases, laying flat on the floor, serving as body armor. The cases sacrificed their exterior shells so the instruments inside could play on, and to Ray and Gabe's great delight, they functioned exactly as intended. The collapse of the roof formed an extra firewall that miraculously prevented the flames from reaching the instruments and making the day a total loss.

Even though there was a silver lining to the vicious and repulsive act by the meth squad, the peeved partners were again left to ponder yet another unexplainable calamity, not of their making, which soon afterward was mitigated by another miraculous event, also not of their making. First, their instruments were stolen and personally returned by the US Border Patrol, and then a fire destroyed their home and everything in it but left their most prized possessions alone. Fate, karma or coincidence?

They dusted off a thick layer of ash and debris from the tops of the cases and yanked them out of the water-soaked rubble they were sitting in. They gasped in unison upon discovering a second surprise hiding underneath. Blackened around the edges, yet still quite legible, were Mr. Gabe's plans, in a pile exactly where his son fortuitously left them. Like

Ray's new acoustic guitar and Gabe's classic saxophone, those plans were destined to be saved. All of that well-intentioned sweat equity Mr. G devoted to planning and designing wouldn't be for nought.

CHAPTER TWENTY-NINE

Ray and Gabe begged the construction crews to put in some major overtime on the new house and finish roofing, framing out, and sheet rocking a couple of rooms to serve as their new temporary shelter because they were a good month or more away from completion and moving in. They incentivized the request by offering them double time and a half in overtime pay and every last one of them agreed.

After the crews left well after midnight, Ray and Gabe sat on the plywood floor, and in the halo of a borrowed Coleman lantern hanging from a rafter, they talked about the growing Christian Science movement, and the virtues of faith, hope, and charity, which Christians of every stripe espouse and strive to practice in their lives. They were both pretty solid on faith and hope, but for Ray especially, the charity part was feeling like it was on shaky ground at that moment in light of their recent encounters with the local tweaker gang. He fumed that they were dreadfully ignorant of the promising future that was in store for them. But how could they be if they never bothered to ask what that future looked like? Instead, they made judgements based solely on the hateful rhetoric that got passed down through generations and then deeply embedded in the tribe's DNA. Ray thought perhaps they don't deserve any of the charity Mr. Gabe had in mind for them. He questioned whether they should keep the farm and deep-six the other plans or cut their losses and leave as unwanted and unsuccessful interlopers.

"But we both know that's not what Jesus would do, right Ray?" Gabe asked. "I hear ya', man. I feel the same. But I keep hearing my father's voice in my head telling me to rise above the hostility. Find some way to make peace. Be the bigger men. Show them what you're made of... goodness and kindness."

"I'm of the mind we somehow show them what they might have had, what could have been, if they had acted differently toward us," Ray threatened. "They should know what they're risking missing out on if we decide to bail on this project."

Dining on saltine crackers and a warm beer, Ray recounted a brief conversation he had with Eagle Eye after the fire in which he reeled off some of the improvements that were planned for the reservation at no cost to them and with no strings attached. He said after the way they'd been treated in their short time there that maybe they should just forget about offering their new neighbors a generous hand up that would guarantee them a better quality of life. Eagle Eye told Ray the tribal council was meeting the following afternoon, and suggested he attend. He might have a chance to inform them they're dangerously close to losing out on the opportunity of a lifetime due to their ignorance and bad behavior.

"That's a tremendous idea! But since we're not tribal members there's no way they would let us in. And then let us speak?" Ray wondered.

Eagle Eye offered a possible workaround to make sure they got their message across and the members heard it loud and clear. He would invite

Ray and Gabe as his guests, which he was permitted by the meeting rules to do, and request a few minutes of member comment time. When his name was called, he would yield his time to his guests. No one had ever tried it, but he felt they had nothing to lose and was optimistic that the council members, whom he knew well, would afford him the courtesy of speaking out as a tribal member.

"I say we give it a whirl and see what happens," Gabe agreed. "If nothing else, we'll get a truer reading on how receptive our neighbors are to outsiders coming in; but more importantly, about breaking out of the status quo and embracing a new and very different way of life, while at the same time, maintaining the tribe's history, culture and traditions."

The following afternoon, the three met up outside the council's offices beforehand and reviewed the strategy a final time before proceeding inside. Eagle Eye noticed Gabe was carrying an armful of rolled up plans and said if those didn't convince the tribe they had only good intentions, then nothing would.

All eyes seemed to laser focus on them when they entered the deadly silent room. There were five tribal council leaders seated around a semi-circular teakwood table at the front facing a seating section with fold-up chairs for about 50 attendees. There were still a few empty seats left when they walked in, so the room was packed full.

Once the usual agenda items had been dispensed with, the public comment period commenced, with a half dozen residents griping about drug dealers, home burglaries, lack of activities for young people, spotty trash collection, and poor animal control.

Next up was Eagle Eye, who approached the council's bench, introduced himself, and declared he was yielding his allotted time to his guests. Ray and Gabe got up and walked from the gallery and stood next to Eagle

Eye. He explained who the two outsiders were and why they came to Dos Cabezas. He chastised those who cast aspersions and rendered judgment on them before knowing the complete and truthful story.

"They're here as my guests today so they can give you the real story, not the one you've been hearing about them running us off the reservation, that is if you're willing to listen," Eagle Eye boldly stated. The council members huddled together for a minute and then announced that it hadn't been properly notified that non-members would be attending and requesting comment time, and consequently wouldn't be permitted to speak at that particular time.

A visibly irritated Eagle Eye snatched the plans out of Gabe's hands and slammed them down on the table with a resounding thud.

He went through them one by one, holding each one up so everyone could see the damage done by the fire and that they miraculously survived.

"This here is a blueprint to build us a brand new school. Imagine that, kids going to school right here on the reservation. This one's for a hospital. This one is for a grocery store, and this is for a house of worship. Look, here's one for a town hall and community center. They wanted to build us a commercial strip mall to start up our own small businesses. And also a treatment center for drug and alcohol addiction. How about a water and waste treatment plant? That smells awfully good to me." That line elicited a few stifled chuckles.

Eagle Eye explained that these improvements, which wouldn't cost them a dime, were part of a master plan to bring natural health and healing to all who truly seek it in their lives. The man who conceived this plan believed the tribe would have been gracious enough to accept these acts of kindness and generosity in the spirit for which they were intended. It presented an opportunity for them to no longer wallow in their pity and to start imagining a better way of life; a life that reflected the ideals and mission of the worldwide health and wellness mecca he wanted to build there. He felt it was essential that the local tribe was included and well-represented, and he put his money where his mouth was. He was willing to invest millions of his personal wealth in their future and for future generations. They were always part of the plan.

Eagle Eye didn't stop there.

"But right away we showed these outsiders just how wrong they were. A few rotten apples trashed their truck and firebombed their trailer to give them an especially warm welcome to the neighborhood," he raged. He concluded by pointing his finger at every person in the room and telling them they can kiss it all goodbye should the partners decide there's no use staying where they're not wanted. Why would they?

A wave of indiscernible, muffled chatter rippled through the seemingly mystified audience, as if this were a revelation to them, which in fact, it was. They had no idea this was in store for them, but Eagle Eye reminded them they didn't give the interlopers a snowball's chance in hell before the hostilities began. Now, it may be too late to un-ring the false alarm bells that went off as soon as the newcomers arrived.

The presenters gathered up the pile of plans and made for the exit straight away, but left Eagle Eye's powerful words to reverberate throughout the room and seep into the bigoted and brainwashed numb skulls who were never taught to think and behave any differently. Instead of the same icy glares and death stares that were directed at them on entering, they were getting faint smiles, more than a few nods of the head, and even some gentle hand clapping. Outside, they just stopped dead in their tracks and smiled at one other. Right then and there, they could see and feel the tide had turned.

CHAPTER THIRTY

Eagle Eye's compelling tribal council presentation was indisputably a game changer for everyone. Everywhere, The mood in general seemed lighter and more neighborly. People offered to pitch in where they could to help finish building the new house so the two men had a place they could actually call home. They brought them food and fixed their meals, built them crude beds so they didn't have to sleep on a cot, helped out with tending to the aloe gardens, and even did their laundry. Ray's name was no longer spoken. Everywhere he went, everybody now referred to him as Aloe Man. His transformation was now complete.

Suddenly, the tribe couldn't do enough to accommodate Ray and Gabe's every need. Their mindset was that by doing so, the partners would succeed at this very arduous labor of love they forfeited their lives for and made a vow to plow until the end of the row. If ever there were a question about leaving or staying, it was clearly answered after their appearance before the tribal council and their victory march afterward. In their minds, it was now full steam ahead; one huge glaring green light signaling all systems go with the plans for Nature's Way Aloe Farm, the Cochise Indian Reservation's numerous enhancements, and the birth of a grand and magnificent entity dedicated to health and wellness named Aloe Valley.

After sipping a sunrise cup of coffee one morning a few weeks later, Ray pulled the bedroom's sliding glass door open and stepped out on the deck. The construction of the two-story house was finally finished but there was still tons of work activity taking place everywhere he looked. It was beginning to sink in that he was actually in charge of it all. He was no longer Raymond Fineman. From here on, he was Aloe Man, and as the man with the plans, he was starting to feel some self-imposed pressure to make sure he got it right after all the promises that were made and the millions that had already been invested in the venture. There were no guaranteed results or outcomes, only promises made that he was hell-bent on keeping.

Gabe joined him on the second-floor deck with a fresh cup of joe, and together they shared a quiet moment to bathe in the glow of the panorama that enveloped them. Ray said nothing and just kept shaking his head, alternately in disbelief and then in utter amazement at the good fortune that was bestowed on him by making this life-altering decision. Now that the project was fully underway and proceeding according to schedule, Ray's anxiety level decreased to the point where he finally was able to process his gratitude to Gabe for making all of it possible. He was never certain up until that moment whether, in the end, he would be grateful for the opportunity, or resentful for luring him away from his little slice of paradise in California and sticking him in a God-forsaken hell hole.

There was still plenty of work to do in preparation for operations to commence and welcome visitors, but they saw progress being made every day, thanks to the dedication of the workforce and the locals who were now just as anxious as Gabe and Ray to see the finished product. Out on the reservation, work had begun on the hospital, the school, treatment plant and the community center, and across the road, Aloe Age Park – which featured the world's tallest bronze sculpture of an *aloe vera barbadensis* with its rejuvenating fountain of youth at the center, and a life-sized sundial – was beginning to take shape.

Where there once was nothing but scorched earth, sagebrush and mangled manzanita, in their place was mineral hot springs, a recirculating waterfall that emptied into a bathing pool below treated with aloe vera gel, several rustic cabins for overnight lodging, and gardens galore: vegetables, herbs, cacti, agave, fruit trees, berries, along with a meditation garden featuring a koi pond, exotic ornamentals, bonsai, topiary, and their two favorite strains of hemp – *cannabis sativa* and *cannabis indica*. Work was scheduled to begin soon on a juice bar, organic food court, and therapy center that offered acupuncture, massage, chiropractic, and revitalizing hot springs and spa treatments.

Ray and Gabe also designed an area for holding drum circles, crystal healing, campfire storytelling, and an old-fashioned band stand where anyone who had the desire to perform, or express their creativity in some way, was free to do so. Performing as the Surf Cowboys, Aloe Man and Gabe were on the bill whenever they chose, which was often in the evenings after sunset. The temperature cooled down slightly and the day's work on the farm and in the park was winding down. It was a pleasant way for them to relax and recharge their batteries.

Over at Nature's Way Farm, the two immense greenhouses were in place, along with a 5,000 square foot production facility where the gel from harvested aloe vera leaves would be extracted under a 100-year-old hydraulic water press formerly used by an apple grower and cider maker in Fly Creek, New York. Ray was amazed first of all that Gabe found such a treasure, and also at the simplicity of its design and environmental friendliness; it used the weight of water to press and extract the precious gel from the leaves, which was then collected and processed for bottling and packaging. Next door, they built two pole barns where a couple of tractors and assorted farm equipment were stored. Two irrigation ponds had been dug. Hiking trails traversed the foothills and mountains, and a spectacular natural rock-climbing wall and performing arts amphitheater were carved out of the solid rock.

Gabe pointed out the obvious: the whole place was buzzing like a beehive. There was furious activity and noticeable progress everywhere. People were suddenly busy rather than bored to tears; they were working, earning a living wage, slowly becoming productive, taking pride in the transformation. They were treating one another more decently, they seemed less angry and bitter now that they had hope and optimism, where a year or two ago there was none, and no prospects on the horizon. There was something to live for rather than mere everyday survival. He couldn't wait for visitors to arrive and enjoy the splendor of Aloe Age Park, which he and Ray designed through pie-in-the-sky conversations about garden attractions, amenities and decor, and then immortalized on the back of a paper plate.

"The key lies in the promotion, Aloe Man," Gabe explained. "We have to let people know we're here If we want them to come visit."

"I was thinking about that too, Gabe. I got this kind of a kooky idea, but it might attract people's attention while they're driving," Ray offered. Gabe was anxious to hear it.

"Do you remember the Burma Shave signs? They used to place them along the roads and highways and on the sides of barns and they used them to advertise their shaving cream with these short, folksy little rhymes that people would read as they traveled around the countryside. I thought that could be a simple way to advertise and it wouldn't cost too much."

"That's a pretty cool idea, Aloe Man. I think people would dig the nostalgia, throwback thing. Those signs were big-time popular back then and sold a ton of shave cream. It was a cheap way to advertise, and they got people talking."

"I even worked out a few rhymes myself," Ray joked. "Wanna' hear 'em? I give you fair warning, they're a little corny."

"I'll be the judge of that. Shoot!" Gabe ordered.

"OK, here we go...

When your moon is blue
And your roses ain't red
Head for Aloe Valley
Better health is just ahead

Health and Wellness
You have to pay to play
Nature's Way's right here
To Save the Day

In a rat race?
Falling behind?
The cure is Aloe Vera
To heal body and mind

A wonderland of healing
To tell you the truth
A modern-day mecca
With a Fountain of Youth"

Gabe guffawed at that last one so loud that he did a spit-take and choked on his beer. A geyser of foam poured out his nose and ran down his chin. Ray didn't know whether he was laughing at how good they were or how bad. Gabe said they were dynamite, and people would love them. They'd have to figure out the best locations and start slicing and dicing through the red tape securing permissions from the appropriate state highway and transportation authorities. Or, they could just go stealth and watch what happened. They'd have to get it together soon because opening day of the park was inching ever closer.

CHAPTER THIRTY-ONE

On the first day of operation, Aloe Age Park entertained 53 anxious, wide-eyed guests. The next day that number grew to 87. By the third day, attendance reached 100, which was the limit that was set so guests had plenty of space to move about freely and maximize their health and healing experience. As it turned out, one hundred visitors a day seemed too sparse, and gave the impression that the park was having difficulty drawing. So they decided to do away with the cap and just take on all comers. They would find a way to accommodate all who made the pilgrimage, who sought them out in pursuit of a healthier way of living. The park was such an enormously wide-open space that it was nearly impossible for anyone to feel crowded or closed in, and there were so many activities to choose from that if one of them was crowded, guests could go do something else and return later.

While Gabe concentrated on the licensing and distribution aspect of Nature's Way products, Aloe Man mainly supervised the planting, maintaining, and harvesting of the farm and gardens, along with monitoring production, but he wanted Ray to become the face of the Nature's Way aloe vera product line, and in his mind, Ray had the potential to easily become the Famous Amos of the aloe world. He was a natural – a healthy and wise old hippie who lived and breathed the product and wanted the whole world to try it and see for themselves. He pictured Aloe Man with a Jesus Christ-like countenance, who wears an aloe vera crown that combines images of Jughead from the Archie comic book series, and auto mechanic Goober Beasley from Andy of Mayberry. Most of all, Aloe Man fit the bill because was a character in every sense of the word.

Aloe Man greeted visitors and led a tour of the Nature's Way farm and production facility each afternoon, and it became one of the more popular attractions. He was full of scientific information, statistics, studies, and supporting literature, and shared it in a friendly, helpful, informal way that endeared him to those on the tour. The lovable lug became a supportive friend and a partner in people's healing process in under an hour. He never forgot a face or a name, and the guests took note of that.

A year in, construction on the reservation's buildings and Aloe Age Park was nearly complete, and the farm was producing aloes the size of which Ray could only have imagined in his wildest dreams. That translated to barrels and barrels of the sacred gel that was processed and packaged, and made its way in the form of bottles, jars and tubes, to drug stores, health food stores, and eventually people's homes. Ray amazed himself every day when he took a moment to realize that he was at the controls of this well-oiled machine and astoundingly it was indeed firing on all cylinders for the most part. He wasn't too proud to acknowledge that Gabe was the real mastermind behind the endeavor and without his herculean efforts, it would have been nothing more than a pipe dream.

By the same token, Gabe felt Aloe Man was equally invaluable because of his botanical knowledge, experience, and eagerness to turn everyone on to aloe vera as a way to achieve optimum wellness of body and mind. Above all, Aloe Man was likable. People saw a lot of themselves in him. He spoke in a way that convinced them there was a better, more natural way to treat their bodies and minds than using over-the-counter medications and prescription drugs. Aloe Man was, in essence, Every Man. He was sick and tired of shameless, profit-hungry drug companies and corrupt, compromised governmental bureaucracies deciding the way people can treat their illnesses, and with medicines only they deem worthy of their approval. Aloe Man felt it was high time to literally put those decisions back in the people's hands and give them a proven alternative therapeutic treatment using a product derived from nature, and not developed in a lab by some chemist.

The reservation was now an entirely different world, too, with retail outlets featuring Native American and boutique clothing and jewelry, a bookstore, and authentic Cochise art, pottery and beadwork that attracted both tribal members and visitors alike. Children walked to and from school, families worshiped and gathered at the community center for Bingo and a game of Canasta. Besides providing greater convenience, the grocery store became a popular meeting and greeting place where locals mingled freely with the visitors. It was easy to tell who was who. Each was eager to learn more about the other. The tribal members weren't accustomed to outsiders, and very few visitors had ever experienced a real life Indian reservation. It was eye-opening and mutually satisfying to say the least.

Aloe Man made it a point to visit the "rez" as often as possible to check on the progress of the building projects and talk with the tribal leaders about any issues they were having. He wanted to get a sense for the tribe's reception to the many drastic changes to their lives and livelihoods and how they were adjusting. During one of those visits, one of the leaders told Aloe Man about an upcoming pow wow and invited him and Gabe to join them. They wouldn't have missed it for the world.

CHAPTER THIRTY-TWO

As they entered the reservation's ceremonial grounds, Gabe recalled he'd been to one of these before but it was eons ago. As a non-native, he wasn't sure he was welcome, but a Native American teacher friend convinced him it was open to any and all with the inclination to experience it. Gabe attended the San Luis Rey Band of the Luiseño tribe's pow wow held on the grounds of a Catholic church in Oceanside, California. His memory was foggy, but he remembered a decent sized crowd and the usual fare one would see at a carnival or street fest – food, beverages, crafts, memorabilia, souvenirs. There was a steady drone of drums beating in the background, and the constant pounding wound up giving him a headache.

That headache vanished when he approached the ceremonial grounds and caught sight of a large group of fully decked out tribal members in their native dress performing a ceremonial dance. They sang songs and chanted, beat on home-made hand drums, and danced maniacally in a colorful circular formation, shaking and convulsing like their bodies had been overtaken by evil spirits. Gabe was fascinated by the elaborate clothing and masks, the feathered headdresses and footwear, and the homemade percussion and wind instruments. Nothing they wore or used was purchased at a store; all of it was made by their skilled hands.

"Sounds pretty rad," Aloe Man said. "I wouldn't mind catching some of that action."

A fair number of visitors streamed in along with tribal members, and a good-sized crowd began forming, which looked encouraging for the vendors, but also gave the tribe a golden opportunity to reach and educate more people as a way to preserve their unique history and put their culture and heritage on full display. Some guests brought lawn chairs, but most people spread out blankets and sat on the ground waiting for the dance ceremony to begin.

When it finally did, the scene played out almost exactly the way Gabe described his pow wow experience in California. Aloe Man was surprised that the dance ceremony of two different tribes could be that similar. As musicians, he and Gabe locked in on the funky polyrhythmic beats they'd never heard before, and were enchanted by the dancers' gruff, percussive chanting in the tribe's native tongue. They couldn't understand the words but somehow their meaning came through in the various intonations the singers produced using only their mouths and collective voices as musical instruments.

When the dance ceremony concluded and they said a final prayer, the leaders of the tribal council came out and one of them, Little Wing, stepped forward and spoke to the hushed assembly.

"Brothers and sisters, it's always a special day when we induct new members into our tribe. The dance you just saw is one that is performed at an induction ceremony. It represents the ecstasy and the overwhelming joy and excitement we feel as part of the same family. It is a life-giving source of energy that comes from our fathers' and their fathers' generations."

"Since we just had the dance, that means we are inducting a new full-blooded member of the Cochise tribe today. For months and months, at every pow wow, we prayed to the Great Spirit to send us a sign that we haven't been abandoned, that there is still hope for us, but we desperately need help. We're hurting and feel we can't crawl out of the deep, dark pit we've fallen into alone."

Well, the Great Spirit graciously heard those prayers and sent us the help and the healing we asked for, and it's sitting right here among us. He sent a miracle worker and a shaman into this valley of darkness and doom and they turned the light back on for us. They brought us an entirely new and different way of life, one that revived the brightness of our souls and made our lives meaningful and worth living.

Today, we honor the work of Gabriel and the tribe's newest shaman, Aloe Man. Please come up and accept these symbols of our everlasting gratitude and love, made with our hands, so that when these come in contact with you, they become one with your spirit."

In total shock and disbelief, Gabe and Aloe Man didn't know what else to do except stand up and do as they were told. They walked to the center of the circle where the council stood and were given a ceremonial tomahawk festooned with feathers and beads, and a beautifully beaded deerskin headband, which the chief placed around their heads and secured. Making the induction official, a drum circle featuring more ceremonial dancing and singing followed, although it now included new members Gabe and Aloe Man the Shaman. At first, they did their best trying to mimic the dancers' steps, but then threw caution to the wind and simply went rag doll.

It was a day they'd always remember. They were completely surprised and impressed that everyone who was in on it was able to keep the secret.

ALOE MAN

Aloe Man in particular was deeply honored that the tribe considered him a healer and medicine man of sorts, which gave a member exalted status and respect in the tribe. And to think only a year or so ago, his truck was destroyed by vandals and the coach he was living in set ablaze. Time does heal all wounds after all.

CHAPTER THIRTY-THREE

The following day broke under gray overcast skies, somewhat of a rarity in the Arizona high desert. There was almost always clear blue skies and bright sunshine to greet the morning, with the occasional rainy and gloomy weather occurring mainly during the winter months. But the calendar read only mid-September, so perhaps the usual pattern was showing up early this year. It wouldn't necessarily have any effect on the gardens unless the temperatures dropped below 40F. If that ever happened, and it did several times over the past century, they'd have a major problem on their hands and could face losing some or all of their aloe crops and fragile flora.

Aloe Man didn't smell the coffee brewing or hear the whirring of the juicer in the kitchen, and then he peeked in Gabe's room and noticed that his bed was already made. He thought Gabe probably rose early and was out working in the pole barn where he set up a small office. He poured two cups of coffee and headed that way. He ran into Eagle Eye and asked if he'd seen Gabe and was told there was no sign of him since before sunrise. Maybe he had errands to run or business to take care of, didn't want to disturb Aloe Man for the keys to his truck, and caught a ride to nearby Bixby with one of the workers. God forbid he ventured out alone somewhere and suffered a heart attack or stroke. He wouldn't survive a day out there.

Aloe Man didn't want to go into panic mode quite yet, but he found Gabe's absence both puzzling and worrisome. Then, a comforting thought eased his mind. Gabe must have walked to the rez to see if anything needed his attention. He was just that kind of guy. He was diligently executing his role as the dutiful son like his father instructed. Aloe Man drove to the general store to inquire whether anyone had seen Gabe. He got a chorus of "Sorry, Shaman" in response. Next, he went to the tribal office in the community center and asked some of the men who were congregating there. Same answer. Now the Shaman was clearly distressed. From what Aloe Man knew about Gabe, doing a disappearing act out of left field, and not leaving a note or telling someone, was unlike him. He did it once before as a surprise, and maybe he was pulling another one out of his hat.

"Was it something I said?" Aloe Man asked himself out loud, half-amusingly and half seriously. "Nah, that's impossible."

They both were positively giddy and praiseful of one another after the pow wow ceremony, so he couldn't have said anything that offended Gabe in that moment. They partied a bit with shots of tequila and some of that high-test reefer Aloe Man referred to as 'da kind." Then the two-fingered guitar wonder and Gabriel the horn blower jammed a few tunes before hitting the sack around midnight.

The council members tried to ease Aloe Man's mind by assuring him they would join in the search as soon as they could. Gabe had only been missing for about 12 hours, so they had to wait another 12 before they could launch an official search. They told Aloe Man the tribe's Chief

Elder, Jahvin, had expressed a desire to meet the shaman at the tribe's sweat lodge, secluded deep in the Dos Cabezas foothills. Aloe Man never knew it existed. They felt the timing was perfect for personal reflection; undergoing the ultimate rejuvenation through a physical and spiritual cleansing of the conscious and subconscious inner-self, designed to purge the body and mind of any bilious toxins that have accumulated within.

Aloe Man was initially hesitant, fearing a trip to a sweat lodge would take his focus off the search for Gabe, although there really wasn't much he could do by himself then and there. On the other hand, the experience may help him relax and clear his head so he could refocus on his search efforts. He also loved the intensity of the sauna-like heat that released any harmful stuff in his body. and the weird effect it had on his breathing. It slowed way down and put him in a calm, peaceful, almost meditative state.

It was about a three-mile hike along a narrow foot trail that led Aloe Man and a leader named Horse Face from the reservation up into the mountains. They reached the sweat lodge encampment where a small cooking fire was burning under a large, black kettle. Judging by the rancid odor emanating from it, what was brewing inside that pot was anyone's guess. They removed their shoes and entered a dimly lit teepee with a small stove, a pile of heated rocks with a bucket of water and a ladle beside it, and an assortment of cowhides covering the floor. Two small ceramic cups sat on a rough-hewn pine table. But no Chief Elder Jahvin.

Horse Face told Aloe Man the chief would be arriving shortly and asked him to kindly strip off his clothing, cover himself with a loin cloth, and sit and wait. Horse Face turned and walked out, leaving Aloe Man alone in the teepee, naked as a jaybird, and with a million thoughts scrambling his brain.

ALOE MAN

A small crack of daylight reflected on the wall of the teepee and in strode the Elder Chief Jahvin by himself. Aloe Man rose and greeted him with a smile and a slight bow. He wasn't sure about handshakes or hugs, so he kept it simple. The lighting was poor, and it was difficult to see, but when they looked at one another, Aloe Man felt that deja vu sensation again, like he was here before, reliving a scene from some time in the past. He told the elder he looked like a Native American chief he saw in a dream. It was a dream about building another man's dream of using nature's way to heal and promote overall good health.

"Not to promote stereotypes, Shaman, but we natives all tend to look the same to people who are non-natives," Jahvin joked. "You probably saw that same face in a John Wayne western, or Wagon Train, or The Lone Ranger and Tonto."

Aloe Man laughed but he knew exactly what Elder Jahvin was talking about, and he was dead on. But he still closely resembled the Indian chief in his dream who looked directly at him and motioned with his hand to follow him into the Aloe Valley. There, he would build an extravagant health and healing center where the only price people paid was choosing to live healthier lives. They chose to pay less for medical bills and price-gouged pharmaceuticals, thanks to nature freely providing equally effective treatments and cures.

They sat down facing one another and Elder Jahvin ladled water on the rocks, instantly creating clouds of steam and raising the temperature to well over 100 degrees. Sweat started pouring off them, which they'd wipe with a towel and then wring out the towel over the rocks, making more steam. Aloe Man was getting a little lightheaded and woozy, but still very much in the moment and enjoying the self-torture. Elder Jahvin handed Aloe Man one of the cups, which contained a lavender tea. He failed to mention it was brewed with hallucinogenic peyote buttons, but Aloe Man suspected the drink would have some mind-altering, consciousness-expanding additive or ingredient.

They drank the magic tea, and it wasn't long before Aloe Man was seeing oddly-shaped hieroglyphic images of buffalos and stick figures dancing on the walls, white hot flashes and streaming trails of light, and everything he looked at appeared as if it were moving fluidly inside a lava lamp. When they spoke, their voices sounded like Alvin and the Chipmunks were speaking. They tried beating hand drums to harness their chi, but their timing went off the rails and they moved on to making shadow puppets on the walls.

Every so often they'd engage in serious conversations about the doctrines of philosophers like Plato and Jung, deep thinking on the ego and existentialism, or Einstein's logic and reasoning behind the age-old question: if a tree falls in the middle of the forest, and no one is there to hear it, does it in fact make a sound? How would one know definitively unless they were actually there. Discuss.

Hours later, when the effects of the magic tea started wearing off, Elder Jahvin saw that Aloe Man still seemed bothered. He asked what was weighing so heavy on his heart and preying on his mind. Aloe Man said he was worried about Gabe. He was nowhere to be found and left without telling anyone.

"Gabe was up here with me this morning," Jahvin said. "Don't sweat it any further, he's just fine. I want to take you up to the mountain top where you'll have a bird's eye view of the farm and the park. You'll be amazed at how it looks from there. It's hard to tell when you're right in the middle of it, but you'll see the incredible work you've done. And Gabe will be there too."

They got dressed and emerged from the teepee, blinded by the bright sunlight and a trifle unsteady on their feet after spending half the day in near darkness in an intensely hallucinogenic state. Aloe Man thought he was still hallucinating when he saw two brown and white spotted palominos tied to a hitching post and saddled up. Deja vu all over again. He remembered seeing that exact image during one of his dreams or flashbacks. Although now it stood right in front of him.

"This is our transportation to the summit, Shaman Aloe Man," pointing to the horses. "Ever ridden a horse?"

Aloe Man laughed and told him about his riding experiences in summer camp, which didn't always work out the way he'd hoped. He enjoyed the feeling he got sitting tall in the saddle and viewing the world from an entirely different perspective. He grabbed his Palomino's reins in one hand and the saddle horn with the other, placed his foot in the stirrup, swung his leg up and over, and set his foot in the other stirrup. That was the moment those same childhood memories and emotions came flooding back.

Chief Elder Jahvin jumped on his horse, whom he named Pal-O-Mine, turned toward the mountain, looked at Aloe Man, and said, "Follow me, Shaman," as he waved his hand in a come-forward motion, just like the dream. Aloe Man felt like he was smacked in the back of the head with a donkey punch. It couldn't be just another coincidence; there had to be some higher power involved in this ongoing series of so-called "coincidences."

CHAPTER THIRTY-FOUR

The way up to the summit of Dos Cabezas was steep and rocky, and no easy going even for the horses. It would have taken half the day hiking it by foot and there was the strong possibility of sprained ankles to boot. The clippity-clop of the horse's hooves against the rocks as they scaled the mountain reminded Aloe Man of his horseback escapades at summer camp. That sound was pure heaven.

When they reached the summit, Gabe was nowhere to be found. Aloe Man was perplexed.

"Where's Gabe?" he asked. "Didn't you say he'd be joining us up here?"

"Indeed, I did, and he's here with us... in spirit," Jahvin replied, smiling.

"In spirit? What does that mean? Did something happen to him that you're keeping from me," Aloe Man demanded to know.

"No, Shaman, I sent him away. His work is finished here," Jahvin said affirmatively.

"What do you mean you sent him away? All due respect, Chief Elder, but what gave you the right to decide his work was done and then ordered him to leave? You're kidding me, right? You're jiving me."

"Gabe works for me, Aloe Man, not you. See, Gabe is my archangel, Gabriel. Remember the surprise delivery of aloes from AG? That was Angel Gabriel. He's one of my very best men, which is why I sent him to help you build the amazing sight you're looking at. But now, Gabe has already moved on to help the next Aloe Man, or whomever I choose to carry out my work here."

"You mean to tell me… you're the Chief I saw in my dream, telling me to come follow you? I knew there was something familiar about you the first time I laid eyes on you! And in the hospital room? No…no….no, you can't be who I think you are!" Aloe Man said, denying the possibility that he and Jesus Christ were on a mountain top together. Or, better still, was this the tail end of the peyote trip he just took in the sweat lodge?

"I am He, Shaman. And yes, I live in every man – the truck driver, the factory worker, the farmer, and yes, the Indian chief. You wondered about your dreams and flashbacks and apparitions, well, wonder no longer. That was the real me appearing to you in reality, although you were in an altered state at the time and were unsure. Yet you took it seriously and heeded the call. You could have written it off, but you believed you were called to do something very special for me and you answered the call even though you had your doubts and your faith was tested many times."

The Elder Chief praised Aloe Man's hard work and grit and told him to carry on as if Gabe were still at his side, because his spirit would be at all times. He pointed toward the cloudless blue sky and declared it was time to go. Dark threatening clouds gathered immediately overhead, and there was an ear-shattering thundercrack followed by a blinding flash of lightning that struck the ground not five feet away. The tremendous force of energy was powerful enough to throw Aloe Man from his saddle and onto the ground, where he smashed his head against a rock and was knocked out momentarily. When he regained consciousness, Elder Chief Jahvin and Pal-O-Mine had vanished into thin air.

Aloe Man stood on the summit alone, concussed and bleeding slightly from his head wound, holding the reins of his palomino, who the Elder named Bonomo. He chose the name because it contained the first four letters for the Latin word "bono" which translates to "good."

Without warning, the wind picked up dramatically and dark clouds gathered and burst open, unleashing sheets of rain that lashed the mountains and the valley below. Within a minute, it drenched the farm and gardens, and the ponds and the mountain streams that were usually a trickle now were deluged with nature's most precious gift. They overflowed, sending cascades of water into the bathing pool below. The thirsty aloes drank their fill, the wildflowers would soon be in full bloom. The pictures in his dreams and apparitions that he visualized were real, and the proof, unless he was still hallucinating or concussed, was right there, clear as day, because he had a hand in every inch of it. This was the real deal.

Aloe Man was shivering and soaked to the bone, but it didn't seem to phase him. He was in a trance observing the full fury of God and nature surrounding him, and realizing that it was a parting gift from none other than his lord and savior. Just then, the rains ceased, the clouds broke, and the sky put on a sunbeam light show. Moments later, a glorious rainbow spread over Aloe Valley, and right then and there Aloe Man found his pot of gold. He wasn't staring at the money; that would all be shared appropriately, and the profits reinvested in perpetuity. Tribal members who were now beginning to study for college and law degrees, thanks to Mr. Gabe's foresight in creating a trust fund for scholarships, would see to that. Aloe Man marveled at his good fortune.

Every year afterward, on that very same date, the exact sequence of events played out in Aloe Valley like clockwork. Dark gray skies, powerful winds, pounding rain, then sunbeams and a dazzling rainbow. It became an annual event that understandably drew people from all over the globe to witness it and Aloe Valley. It was a certifiable miracle – like those that took place at Lourdes or Fatima or Guadalupe – and occurred with such regularity that travel and vacations were planned around the date. It was, for lack of a better word, a spectacle – a huge gathering in the desert where wellness-minded people came to witness the grandeur and harmonic convergence of the spiritual and natural worlds, and to recharge their dying or dead batteries at the same time.

For Aloe Man, it was, upon deeper reflection, a succession of tiny miracles over the course of his life that brought him to this place and moment in time. But none of those added together could ever compare to the magnificent Miracle at Aloe Valley. The Great Spirit in the sky made sure of it.

Every once in a while, in the ensuing days and weeks and months, Aloe Man felt an odd sensation that someone or something was eyeballing him, shadowing him and even peering over his shoulder while he worked. Then he'd hear a saxophone playing in his head and realize his guardian angel Gabe was close by and watching over him.

He often wondered how in the world he ever got to this place. He never dreamed of becoming Aloe Man. Like most youngsters, his dreams of what he wanted to be when he grew up were pretty average. At first, he wanted to be a banker because his father worked at one. That soon changed to playing professional football or baseball because he was quick, becoming a newspaper photographer because he thought Jimmy Olsen on Superman had a cool job, or a phys ed teacher because he didn't really have to teach and had summers off.

None of those dreams came true, mostly because real life events were thrown into the mix and shook things up. To a large degree, they steered his future course and instead of his original aspirations, he became a musician, a Good Humor man, a drug rehab patient-turned-counselor, a gardener, a shaman, a farmer, and a wellness advocate.

Unbeknownst to him, paths that he never could have imagined led him to the present day. He may have thought he was in full control of his destiny, but now he realized he never was. He was predestined to become Aloe Man. That was the reason why he was created and the true purpose of his existence. It was the work for which he was best suited.

The Angel Gabriel, with the grace of God and by doing his will, turned Raymond Fineman into Aloe Man. Gabe placed him behind the wheel and brought him to Aloe Valley. He demonstrated to Aloe Man the power of faith, both in God and in oneself; the virtue of resilience; the value of respect and listening before making up one's own mind; of recognizing that us souls were placed here on this earth for a purpose; that God didn't create us to do nothing with our lives.

Aloe Man found it hard to believe at one time he was an aspiring rock star, the love of his life committed murder and then was murdered, his brother took his own life, he got busted and did time in a drug rehab, and lost three fingers in a tree-pruning accident. All of that tragedy combined miraculously transformed him into an entirely new and different person. He assumed a brand-new persona as the face of Nature's Way and Aloe Valley, and he embraced every aspect of it. His passion for and dedication to the work for which he was chosen earned him the title of Aloe Man and shaman. He didn't bestow it on himself. He considered it God-given.

Unashamedly throwing out the hang loose sign, he walked about the park wearing a tee-shirt emblazoned with a giant "A" on the front similar to Superman's notorious "S." Aloe Man wasn't claiming to be a Superman with super healing powers. The only superpowers he possessed were those that came from above and delivered him to that sacred place. Those were powers that made Aloe Man the real man he was destined to be.

About the Author

Richard Michael Barrett is a multifaceted writer, editor, and photojournalist, with a rich portfolio that spans newspapers, magazines, and online platforms. His career has seen him working in print and broadcast media, corporate communications, and advertising. Richard's creativity extends beyond journalism, as he is also a children's book author, playwright, poet, lyricist, and musician. Some of his children's books include *Farmer Fred Feeds His Friends* and *Sylvester the Fox Wants a Job at the Zoo*. A lover of the outdoors and culinary arts, Richard resides in German Flatts, NY, sharing his home with his dog, Jet.